The 25 Pains
of Kennedy Baines

The 25 Pains
of Kennedy Baines

Dede Crane

RAINCOAST BOOKS

Vancouver

Raincoast Books gratefully acknowledges the ongoing support of the Canada
Council for the Arts, the British Columbia Arts Council and the Government of
Canada through the Book Publishing Industry Development Program (BPIDP).

Edited by Elizabeth McLean
Cover and interior design by Teresa Bubela

Library and Archives Canada Cataloguing in Publication

Crane, Dede
   The 25 pains of Kennedy Baines / Dede Crane.
ISBN 10 1-55192-979-1
ISBN 13 978-1-55192-979-8
   I. Title. II. Title: Twenty-five pains of Kennedy Baines.
PS8605.R35T84 2006 jC813'.6 C2006-902384-0

Raincoast Books   In the United States:
9050 Shaughnessy Street   Publishers Group West
Vancouver, British Columbia   1700 Fourth Street
Canada V6P 6E5   Berkeley, California
www.raincoast.com   94710

Raincoast Books is committed to protecting the environment and to the responsible use of natural resources. We are working with suppliers and printers to
phase out our use of paper produced from ancient forests. This book is printed
with vegetable-based inks on 100% ancient-forest-free paper (40% post-consumer
recycled), processed chlorine- and acid-free. For further information, visit our
website at www.raincoast.com/publishing.

Printed in Canada by Webcom.

10 9 8 7 6 5 4 3 2 1

To those who constantly inspire me, and in this order:
Lise, Connor, Vaughn and Millicent.

Kennedy can't say exactly when the psychoshift happened, only that she used to see life as a pretty positive thing. Now she can't stop seeing it as one pain after another.

PAIN #1: SHOPLIFTING

Why is this considered a fun thing to do?

"Hurry up, you guys, I'm thirsty," says Sarina, though Kennedy knows she doesn't mean it.

"Go get your Slurpee then," sneers Chase, all part of the ploy.

"Fine, I will." She palms a Kit Kat.

Kennedy figures that Sarina, who's got more than enough spending money, does it for the rush. Chase has some anti-capitalist logic about "undermining the system," but she thinks his real reason is being broke and too proud to borrow money. Kennedy's boyfriend, Jordan, who's terminally hungry and a sugar addict, probably does it to please Chase. And perhaps to impress her. Kennedy does it simply because these are her friends. Lame but true.

Jordan grabs a Mr. Big bar and Chase laughs out loud.

"Shut up," hisses Jordan, laughing too. He tucks the candy bar under his arm.

Kennedy shoots them a look. Being taller than all her friends, even Jordan, she already feels she stands out like a red flag. And her hair is frizzing so badly in this hot weather, her head must be twice its normal size. She glances up at the turbaned guy unpacking cigarettes behind the front counter. Every few minutes, like a reflex, he glances up at the TV camera. One of four shots is aimed at the candy aisle. Kennedy is doing her best to block the camera's view.

They had agreed out in the parking lot which two of them would buy "the front candy." Rule one is to make purchases. Kennedy always volunteers to be a candy buyer because it feels safer. And this time Chase volunteered for a change. While she's working up her nerve, Chase hand-picks three five-cent cinnamon lips into a bag, holds it up and makes a big show of recounting them.

Opposite the candy are layers of magazines, the covers glossy with skin and big-breasted women clothed mostly in tough chick smiles. Kennedy tries on her own tough chick smile and after Chase slips a Snickers up his shirt sleeve, she steps in front of him to switch places. Her smile dissolving, she picks out the smallest thing there, Rollos, and, because it's easiest, takes two. She hides one in her palm, lets the other show. They wander over to Sarina at the Slurpee machines.

Rule two is to keep talking. Jordan asks who's going to Miko's tomorrow night.

"I think Brice is coming. And Graham," says Chase.

"Graham and Willow still going out?"

"Far as I know."

Kennedy's too nervous to do more than listen.

They get their Slurpees and all go up to the cash together. Rule three is to leave as a group. As Kennedy waits in line behind Sarina, her heart is pounding so loud in her ears she assumes others can hear it too.

"God, it's hot," says Sarina. "Maybe we should walk up to the new water park."

Kennedy nods, her throat too constricted to speak. Sarina pays and it's Kennedy's turn. She puts the drink and single pack of Rollos on the counter, then digs in her pocket for money. Her fumbling hand drops a quarter noisily to the floor. Jordan, behind her, picks it up and puts it on the counter.

"Thanks," says Kennedy, her voice no more than a whisper. Funny that she's the nervous one here, she thinks, looking at Jordan. Usually it's the other way around.

Catching the cashier's expressionless eye, Kennedy gives the woman her money and a friendly smile, then instantly feels like a two-faced jerk. She wonders if this man and woman own the store, perhaps have invested their life savings. She looks down at her hand resting on the counter. It's shaking. She picks up her purchases and, not trusting her hands to hold two things at once, fits the candy into the pocket of her shorts.

"Keep the change," she says when the woman hands back her change.

The woman says nothing, only drops it into the take one, leave one tray.

Kennedy steps ahead, then glances back at Jordan about

to put his Slurpee on the counter. Under the transparent lid, the bright yellow tip of the Mr. Big bar is sticking right up out of the green slush. Kennedy lurches forward and grabs the Slurpee out of his hands.

"Let me taste yours," she blurts, tipping the cup toward her face and away from the cashier.

"A large," says Jordan to the woman and hands over his money.

"Mmm, I should have gotten that," Kennedy says, talking way too fast. She feels heat rising in her face.

She doesn't hand back his Slurpee until Jordan is well away from the counter. Chase is paying for his stuff now, his eyes teary from suppressed laughter.

It's not until they're out of the store and around the corner that Chase breaks down laughing. "God, it was poking right out of the top," Chase coughs through his laughter. He grabs Jordan's cup. "Look at that nob sticking up."

"Don't talk nasty," says Sarina.

Jordan laughs and blushes at the same time.

"Kennedy saved your ass," says Chase.

"All of our asses," corrects Sarina. "You're our hero, Kennedy."

Sarina, who comes up to Kennedy's shoulder, leans over and kisses Kennedy on the arm. Kennedy is too intent on keeping everyone walking to absorb any praise. She's imagining the turbaned guy running up behind them holding a baseball bat, a police car cutting them off at the corner. She can't relax until they've reached the skateboard park behind the school.

As they settle on the grass, Chase waves to a couple of skater friends.

"Effective but messy," says Sarina, hauling a dripping Kit Kat from her cup.

Sarina sounds so unfazed, Kennedy has to wonder if no one gets freaked out except her. The fact that they've done the Slurpee trick three times now doesn't make it any less nerve-wracking because, as she figures it, the chances of getting caught are only going up.

"Shoplifting makes me so nervous," says Kennedy, letting go a big breath.

"The worst they'll do is try and scare you," says Jordan.

"What about that time Graham got caught stealing a magazine? The police took him to the station and put him in a cell," says Sarina.

"Yeah, for about as long as it took for his dad to come get him," says Chase.

"I hear if it's your first offence they let you go and the record's erased when you turn eighteen," says Kennedy. "But if it's your second offence, you can lose your right to leave the country. For good." Kennedy had researched it on the net.

"Weird rule," says Sarina. "You'd think they'd *want* you to leave the country."

The fact that first offenders get off lightly is Kennedy's only solace in this shoplifting game. She knows Mom would just chalk it up to being fifteen, possibly one-up her with her own shoplifting story. But Dad ... Dad would be so disappointed. She can imagine him picking her up at the police station, looking confused and hurt. The thought makes her chest go hollow. She leans back against Jordan's shoulder, wishing he'd put his arm around her, wishing he instinctively know she needed comforting.

She smiles up at him. He smiles shyly over his straw, then makes a sloppy slurping noise as he drinks. He suddenly looks eleven. Sighing, she reaches into her cup for her slush-slimed candy.

"Anybody want a Rollo?"

2

Kennedy turns onto her side and studies the cat's head as it yawns, amazed at the long blade-like incisors next to front teeth tiny as a doll's. Petting Mojo's soft head, Kennedy realizes his skull isn't round but shaped like a large clam. She squints over at the clock. Ten-thirty. So great to sleep in now that school's out. Being startled awake by an alarm has got to be unhealthy, she muses, damaging even, the way it rips you out of a dream before you're ready. Like surfacing too quickly from a dive.

PAIN #2: CANKLES

Kennedy reaches her size nine feet toward the ceiling, examines her long, muscled legs, which would be pretty nice except for her shapeless ankles as big around as her calves. She runs her hand along her shin and feels tiny bristles. Should shave before the party tonight. Sarina and Miko will be sleeping over. The whole thing was supposed to be at Miko's, but now it's here because Miko's mother is suddenly "unwell." Kennedy knows Miko's parents get uneasy when Miko has more than two people over.

"So many friends," they say, their tongues flattening

the difficult r. Having come from Japan only six years ago, Miko's parents find it hard to be outnumbered by foreigners in their own house. Miko had called last night to see if Kennedy could have it at her place.

Kennedy hasn't asked her parents yet, but she will — ask her mom, that is. Mom almost never says no. In fact, she seems vicariously thrilled that her daughter *has* a social life. But Kennedy hates having parties at her house because then she's the one "in charge," which means it's much harder to relax and have a good time. She doesn't know why Sarina couldn't have it at her place. It's her turn. Besides, her house is bigger than anybody's, has a pool table and a giant TV screen. And unlike Kennedy, Sarina doesn't have a younger brother and baby sister around to bug them. Sarina hasn't had people over to her place like forever, thinks Kennedy, trying not to feel resentful. Her stomach growls with hunger.

Oh well, Jordan will be here. She kicks at her covers. He obviously likes her a lot and she thinks she likes him. He's almost as tall as her, rare among the boys her age, and he's really cute, pimples aside. But god, he's shy. They've been "going out" for a month now and he hasn't even kissed her other than a peck on the lips. Of course, she's waited for *him* to initiate things. Tonight, she'll simply get Jordan alone and kiss him for real. Some guys probably just need to get jump-started. She gives the cat's clamhead one last pet, puts on her glasses and climbs out of bed.

Kennedy makes her way through the rec room to the bathroom, washes her face and tugs a comb through her long mess of curls. As she often does, she assesses her face. Okay hair when it doesn't frizz on her, which it does all summer long. Full enough lips, nice eyes — super blue like Dad's ... she stops and sighs, staring at her long, pointed nose, the nose that insists on ruining it all. She hears her mother's voice. "You wouldn't want to be more pretty than you already are. Not with your figure." True, she has a good body, thinks Kennedy, even her friends say so. Cankles and giantness aside.

Kennedy ties back her unruly curls, decides against contacts, goes to her room for her book, then heads upstairs.

Though Kennedy likes the privacy of her new room in the basement, away from the rest of the family, sometimes it feels as if she's been relegated to the lower realms and forgotten. Nobody bothers to come downstairs and say good morning, ask if she slept well, if she wants anything special for breakfast. She has to go to them. If she didn't go upstairs some morning, she wonders how long it would take for someone to seek her out.

The other thing she doesn't like about her basement room is that every summer, spiders are everywhere. Huge, black skittery wolf spiders, the size of your hand. Spiders freak her out. Spiders look like evil sounds. She heard on the radio that we ingest approximately three spiders a year. This disgusting act is supposed to happen in our sleep, when the spiders are inhaled nasally or orally, depending if you're a mouth breather or nose breather. Kennedy imagines a wolf spider's thumb-sized body stuck halfway up one of her nostrils and takes the stairs two at a time.

PAIN #3: TORY

Just before Christmas, Tory moved out of Mom and Dad's room and took over what used to be Kennedy's room upstairs. Kennedy never once saw a spider in that room.

It's the nicest room in the house, really, considering it has its own balcony. Kennedy likened the balcony to the one off Juliet's room in *Romeo and Juliet*, only made from cedar instead of Italian stone. Four years ago, when they moved here from Fredericton, New Brunswick, Kennedy and her mom had planted rose bushes along the balcony's supports, hoping to train them to branch up the balcony wall and trim the ledge with flowers. The leaves got eaten by something and died. Slugs, most likely, Dad said. The west coast is loaded with slugs. "Homeless snails," as her brother Liam calls them.

Upstairs in the living room, Tory's watching a *Blue's Clues* video. The dried remains of chicken pox mar her four-year-old face and make Kennedy think of Jordan's acne. Tory calls them her "chicken pops."

"You know Blue's buddy there, Steve, killed himself," says Kennedy, motioning to the TV. She watches Tory's eyes shift from complacency to confusion. "Probably took his safety scissors, cut his finger off and bled to death." She snips across her finger with imaginary scissors.

Tory glances up at Kennedy to determine whether or not her big sister's joking, and a look of sad panic comes over her pocked face.

Kennedy watches Tory's eyes film over and tries not to cringe inside.

"Mommy," Tory yells, and runs toward the faint reply from the laundry room. The pink tulle of her ballerina skirt brushes past Kennedy's bare leg, causing a shiver to snake up her spine.

Why do I have to do that? Kennedy scolds herself, suddenly no longer hungry, which is why she came upstairs in the first place. She'll have to apologize; besides, it's not true. There was a rumour going around MSN that he'd offed himself, but Miko checked out his website and it was just a hoax.

Tory comes sniffling back into the living room.

"Mom says he didn't," Tory says with paper-thin confidence.

"She's right, Tor, I was only kidding. Sorry." And she is sorry for torturing such a small brain.

"You're mean now," Tory states simply, as if resigned to the fact, and resettles herself in front of her show.

Kennedy sulks off to the kitchen. It's true, she was nicer last year, even last month. Maybe the pyschoshift happened when she turned fifteen. Since her birthday, it seems that unspoken, even unconscious resentments, from birth onward, have been seething to the surface. She doesn't really hate her family, not deep down, but in the moment she can't seem to help herself. Her anger feels biological and if she doesn't express it, she'll blow some sort of fuse. She doesn't hate her dad, though, she could never hate him. He's too ... vulnerable.

Liam is at the kitchen counter eating cereal out of a beer mug. Thirteen years old, with brown hair, white-blond eyebrows, a freckled nose (when nothing else is freckled), and ears too small for his head, Liam looks like he was pieced together wrong. Like Tory's Mr. Potato Head. Kennedy would give anything for his nose, though, minus the freckles.

"Hey teammate, teammate-for-life," says Liam, speed-talking the way he does. "I'm changing my name to Mullet."

Kennedy just looks at him, pictures his brain as a spinning top.

"Call me Mullet," Liam says through a mouthful of Frosted Flakes.

Rolling her eyes, she opens the fridge.

"Mullet Baines," he tries out the name. "Kennedy meet Mullet. Mullet, Kennedy."

"I wish you'd get those pictures of guys with mullets off the screen saver. It's too gross." She looks for the cream cheese but it's not in its normal place.

"It's funny. Funny meet Kennedy, who's not funny. Kennedy meet funny, who is hella funny."

Mom comes into the kitchen carrying a pile of folded dishcloths. Recently she cut her shoulder-length hair off, all the way off, as in practically shaved it, leaving only some token bangs behind. And now that her "figure's come back," she's started dressing differently too. Instead of loose-cut pants and a collared shirt, or one of her long cotton dresses, she's wearing fitted black jeans and a T-shirt that shows loose belly skin when she lifts her arms. It just looks wrong. Like she's desperate to be young again or something.

"Don't forget to put your dishes in the dishwasher when you're finished eating, please," says Mom. "And you should both have a piece of fruit with your breakfast. The pears are ripe."

"Sure, mother-poppin-no-breathing," spins Liam. "Pears it is, if you let me change my name to Mullet."

Mom laughs. Kennedy has no idea where he gets his expressions from or even what they mean half the time. Is her mother wearing mascara?

"Tory's still contagious for another day or two," says Mom, "so I need one of you to babysit while I go to my audition for that play."

Kennedy pretends not to have heard her.

"That's cool, way cool, play cool," says Liam. "But I babysat yesterday, M-Dot. It's Kennedy's turn."

"Kennedy?" Mom turns to her. "If I leave now, I'll be back around one."

"Fine, okay," she says, keeping her head inside the fridge. She can't look at her mom with that haircut and in that outfit. She rummages through the shelves, knowing the cream cheese container was nearly full yesterday.

"Thanks." Mom lowers her voice. "Did the guy on *Blue's Clues* really kill —"

"That was just a stupid rumour," pipes up Liam.

"Oh good. That wasn't very nice, Kennedy," says Mom.

"I already apologized."

"Okay, I'm off. See you shortly."

"Uh, Mom?" she says.

"Yes?"

"Is it all right to have some people over tonight and a couple friends sleep over after?" For once Kennedy wishes the answer would be no.

"Sure, honey, as long as you girls clean up after yourselves."

"Thanks," Kennedy mumbles, finally locating the cream cheese behind the ketchup. Great, the downstairs is a pigsty, so she'll be cleaning up before and after the party. She slams the fridge door so hard the house shakes.

"Kennedy's having a hissy fitty," says Liam, and hisses a sustained "Ssss" into his beer mug.

"Shut up." Kennedy snatches up a bagel.

She hears Mom kiss Tory goodbye, Tory whining that she wants Liam to babysit, not Kennedy.

PAIN #4: BABYSITTING

Kennedy was in grade five when her mother got "accidentally pregnant" at age thirty-nine. It was embarrassing. Then her mother openly breast-fed until Tory was three. Three! Kennedy had no choice but to stop inviting friends around. Mom's never had much in the way of modesty, hardly ever shuts the door when she's in the bathroom, while Kennedy's the opposite, more like her father. Kennedy's friends, though, all think her mom's cool because she's more open-minded than other parents. She likes that part okay, but sometimes her mom goes too far. Like last week, when she tried to put a bowl of condoms in Kennedy's bathroom.

"What? Why?" was all Kennedy could manage.

"My friend Marie-Anne keeps a bowl in her Pierre's bathroom and has trouble keeping it filled. It's just so you and your friends have easy access to protection. It's the ones who —"

"Then I'll tell them to go hit up Pierre's bathroom," she'd said, handing back the bowl. God, guys would think she was asking for it. What was her mother thinking?

"I shoddy the computer," calls Liam. "Got a Counterstrike match in two minutes sharp. A Clan match," he says. "Manny versus Mullet. The fans will be there, mullets groomed and gelled. Mullet gel. Hey, why doesn't mullet rhyme with bullet? Mullet, bullet. Mullet, bullet."

Kennedy escapes her brother's mindless chatter to eat her bagel out on the deck. She can't stand not to read while eating and opens her book, *Pride and Prejudice*. She's reading it for the third time. She's read all of Jane Austen's novels, even *Sanditon*, the one Austen started before she died and never finished. Kennedy loves how *Sanditon* was finished off by a woman who declined to use her real name and that the cover reads "by *Jane Austen and Another Lady.*"

Kennedy likes all of Austen's books, but *Pride and Prejudice,* by far, has the best characters and the most romantic plot. She gets lost in the gentle pace of life back then, the formality of the language, and she can hear the musical English accents. She has wanted to reread it ever since her mom brought home the movie from the library — the BBC version with Colin Firth. Colin Firth, number one English hunk. Her friends think she's nuts, thinks she has a fetish for older men which she doesn't. They all love Heath Ledger, Chad Michael Murray, Orlando Bloom. She does think Orlando is okay and he's English too, but he doesn't have Colin's shy grace and brooding. She can't believe they made a new version of *Pride and Prejudice* starring Keira Knightley. Why? Why? When the BBC version is already perfect. Kennedy had Googled the new movie to see who played Mr. Darcy and it was some pasty-faced guy with a fat nose whom she'd never heard of. He looked grubby, his hair all dishevelled. Mr. Darcy is not dishevelled. She never wants to see it, not even on video, afraid it will ruin the book for her, wreck the images in her mind from the BBC version.

She takes another bite of bagel and then stops chewing. She's come to the part in the book when, at a ball at Meryton, Mr. Bingley — a rich Londoner who recently purchased an estate in the area — tries to get his snooty friend Mr. Darcy to join in the dancing. Mr. Bingley offers to have his dance partner Jane introduce Darcy to her sister Elizabeth, who is near enough to overhear his reply: *"She is tolerable; but not handsome enough to tempt me; and I am in no humour at present to give consequence to young ladies who are slighted by other men. You had better return to your partner and enjoy her smiles, for —"*

"Kendy." A thorn from another world.

PAIN #5: KENDY

It always sounds like Tory's saying "Candy."

"What is it?"

"My movie's over. I want you to play Snakes and Ladders with me."

"Aaaach ...Take me away from here," she says through clenched teeth. She hears Liam's computer game explosions, his grunts of victory. "If only I'd been born an only child in nineteenth-century England. In a minute," she calls, trying to relocate her place in the book.

"Hurry," urges Tory. "One of my chicken pops is coming off."

Mom arrives home at ten after two, more than an hour later than she'd promised. Over the course of the last three hours, Kennedy has made one snack for her little sister, lunch and some lemonade that Tory promptly spilled all over herself. She has played one game of Snakes and Ladders and two games of Candyland, pushed her sister on the swing for what felt like eternity, and filled in a half dozen paint-by-number pictures. This last activity, though, was mind-numbing to the point of being soothing and Kennedy was almost loath to stop. On her way downstairs to start cleaning, she wonders why life couldn't come with such simple, numbered directions.

She grabs her CD player to put in the bathroom so she'll have music to clean by. It's the one downfall of having her own bathroom. Cleaning it. She picks out one of her CDs that she likes to sing to because singing makes any task bearable and the acoustics in her windowless bathroom are excellent. Since cleaning toilets requires uplifting music, she chooses the pop-opera star Sarah Brightman — whom she only dares listen to when her friends aren't around.

She loves listening to Andrea Bocelli too, and Céline Dion, singers whose voices give her chills, and whose CDs she hides under her bed.

Bent over a tubful of Comet, Kennedy harmonizes her alto with Sarah Brightman's soprano, trying to "place the high notes on the ground" like Aunt Cathy used to instruct her to do. Aunt Cathy, her father's sister, was the choir teacher in Kennedy's school back in Fredericton. She gave Kennedy private singing lessons on the side. Though Victoria feels like her home now, Kennedy still misses her aunt, her grandparents and her old best friend Martha, whom she's seen only once since the move. Kennedy's dad, born and raised in Fredericton, wasn't too happy about leaving his family and friends. At the time, neither was Kennedy.

She stops singing and scrubs angrily at the green scum around the drain hole. Something happened back then that Kennedy has tried to forget ever since. Lately, though, the memory keeps flashing in her head like a gross-out scene in a movie you covered your eyes too late for. Back in Fredericton, Mom worked part-time in a funky consignment store and performed every spring with a local theatre group. Kennedy used to collect the programs from her mom's plays, underlining her name, Leslie Baines, with a yellow highlighter. She'd feigned sick the night her dad and Liam went to see this particular play and threw away the program Dad brought home for her.

She and Liam had gotten out of school early one day because of a bad smell in the school connected to a gas leak. She walked with Liam to the Playhouse, where she knew her mother was rehearsing. It was just after one o'clock and the actors must have been on a break because the stage was empty. Kennedy made Liam sit in the theatre while she wandered backstage to find Mom. And she found her all right, in one of the dressing rooms, with her arms and lips around the director. And it wasn't just a friendly kiss, either. In fact, it was still going on during the time it took Kennedy to close her mouth and move silently away from the door.

Mom didn't see Kennedy and Kennedy never mentioned it. To anyone. Not to Martha, not to Dad, no one. She had taken Liam, walked home and stayed there alone until Mom arrived, despite the fact that she was under the legal age to babysit.

So Kennedy still wonders if there was another reason Mom was so eager to move.

PAIN #6: DOUBT

Lately Kennedy has started to put two and two together. It seemed that it wasn't very long after she witnessed that kiss that Mom announced she was pregnant. And then, not long after that, she started going on about some fisheries job in Victoria and wouldn't let it go until Dad applied for it. The baby, named Tory — short for Victoria — was born a week after Dad learned he'd got the job. Tory, come to think of it, doesn't really look like her or Liam. Luckily she looks a lot like Mom, though Tory's hair is much darker than everyone else's. Kennedy can't remember for sure the hair colour of the director, has blocked it out, but believes it's black, black as night.

Dad has never seemed the least bit suspicious of Mom. But then Dad isn't the suspicious type. He's trusting and soft-spoken, and he gives people the benefit of the doubt.

He doesn't ask too many questions. Kennedy's the one with too many questions — though she doesn't exactly ask them. Since the move, Mom has stayed at home with Tory and Kennedy has stopped worrying. But a few weeks ago Mom met a woman at the playground who's involved in a theatre group here in Victoria. Now she has cut off her hair, is wearing tight jeans and auditioning for some play, and the worry's starting all over again. Kennedy shakes her head to try and lose the picture of her mother and that man.

Tipped upside-down over the tub, she focuses on singing and remembers how Aunt Cathy used to make her repeat her voice exercises while hanging upside-down "in order to free your upper range." As the song nears its end, she straightens up and takes a deep breath before striking the final high note. Kennedy holds the note just as long as Brightman and feels a tingling at the crown of her head. The sensation is new to Kennedy, yet it's exactly how Aunt Cathy used to describe "high notes finding their home." The sound resonates with a kind of bright contentment, thinks Kennedy, like a tiny sun. She comes to the end of her breath and reluctantly lets the note go, the pleasurable feeling in her head fading with it. She proceeds to rinse out the tub before starting on the toilet, eager for the next song, "Requiem," to start, so she can try and recapture the feeling.

Bathroom finished, Kennedy takes a shower, washes her hair and shaves her legs. Afterwards she combs out her wet hair with anti-frizz cream, then flops down on her bed with *Pride and Prejudice*. She reads up to the second ball, the one at Sir William's where Elizabeth gets back at Mr. Darcy by refusing his sincere offer of dancing. Mr. Darcy is taken aback by the rejection as well as taken with Elizabeth when Mr. Bingley's conceited sister, who has serious designs on Mr. Darcy, sidles up to him: *"I can guess the subject of your reverie."*

"I should imagine not."

"You are considering how insupportable it would be to pass many evenings in this manner — in such society; and indeed I am quite of your opinion. I was never more annoyed! The insipidity and yet the noise: the nothingness and yet the self-importance of all these people! — What would I give to hear your strictures on them!"

"Your conjecture is totally wrong, I assure you. My mind was more agreeably engaged. I have been meditating on the very great pleasure which a pair of fine eyes in the face of a pretty woman can bestow."

So romantic, thinks Kennedy, patting her chest over her heart.

When Miss Bingley asks which woman he's referring to — hoping it's herself — he replies *"with great intrepidity, 'Miss Elizabeth Bennet.'"*

Kennedy will have to look up the word *intrepidity*. She lowers the book and thinks how exciting courtship sounded in the nineteenth century. They chose their words so carefully that language itself was like a dance, one person leading, another following, both watching for a misstep. A touch of the hand or waist was as intimate and thrilling as a kiss. A kiss, thinks Kennedy, which never happens in Jane Austen's novels, must have been too intoxicating for words. Kennedy sighs. Back then, sex was not even a consideration until marriage. Now sex is always in the background. It's not only a question of when you're

going to do it, but there seems to be a right and a wrong
way to do it. Kennedy can hear Mom going on about
"making friends with your clitoris."

PAIN #7: MOM'S LITTLE TALKS

Mom tries to force these "little talks"on Kennedy about
sex and birth control — "now," she likes to preface them
with, "before it becomes an issue ..." But talking about
sex with her mother icks her out. And what can her mom
know about birth control when her little "accident" is
upstairs colouring all over the walls in Kennedy's old bedroom. Besides, people have been doing *it*, like, forever.
Birth control aside, you'd think sex would just come
naturally, without having to think about it. Kind of like
sneezing.

Kennedy lifts her book up off her chest, but the words
go fuzzy on the page. Life today seems so crude compared
to two hundred years ago. Shouldn't we be getting more
refined, not less? She can't imagine a conversation with
any of the boys she knows being in any way emotionally
satisfying. Guys never talk about real things, like their feelings or their dreams. It's not cool. Just to be held and
kissed by a boy who's not afraid to hold her and kiss her
would be fine for now. Sometimes her body seems to be
screaming to be touched by another's hands. A feeling no
different from needing water or food. But then she wants a
physical relationship that's meaningful too. Oh god, she
doesn't know what she wants. Life was so much simpler in
Austen's time with all its taboos.

"I'm so confused," Kennedy says to the ceiling. She rolls
onto her side to stare out the window at an empty blue sky.
"What do I want?"

Soon after dinner, Sarina arrives to help Kennedy clean up the rec room for the party. Sarina's wearing her new Gap shirt and capris plus a white jacket that Kennedy hasn't seen before. Sarina has the most up-to-date wardrobe of any of their friends. What with Mom not working and B.C. being that much more expensive than the Maritimes, money's tight and most of Kennedy's clothes are from second-hand stores. Mom calls second-hand shopping recycling; says we're helping to save the planet's resources. Fine, but as a result Kennedy's flares are always a little too flared or not flared enough, her shirts last year's colours, her shoes all wrong.

"When did you get the jacket?" asks Kennedy.

"Good ol' mommy took me shopping this afternoon. Guilt shop for being out of town all last week."

"Boy, she travels a lot."

"Yeah," Sarina says, her green eyes flickering dark. "The Emily Carr exhibit's on tour right now."

"She bought you shoes too?" says Kennedy, noticing Sarina's black patent-leather, spike-heeled sandals.

Sarina, only five feet tall, always wears heels and has more shoes than all of their friends put together. She and Kennedy are forever wishing they were three inches taller and shorter respectively.

"Yeah, and a couple of CDs." She raises her eyebrows. "Got Green Day's new one."

"Great. Put it on."

"But first," says Sarina, pulling a large bottle from her bag, "where should I hide this?" She does a pirouette, stops, and gives the bottle a loud smacking kiss. "Bacardi Rum," she says, reading the label. The bottle's not quite full and

Kennedy has to wonder if Sarina's been at it already.

"Where did you get it?"

"Stole it from my grandmother's liquor cabinet. It's probably been in there for like eighty years. Does liquor go bad?"

Kennedy shrugs. "How would I know?"

"Where should I put it?"

"In my closet, I guess," says Kennedy. "Man, that bottle's big enough."

"Yeah, but I don't know what *you* guys are going to drink."

Kennedy laughs and Sarina unscrews the cap, takes a substantial swig, then coughs into her sleeve. "Want a hit?"

"I'll wait," says Kennedy, again wishing the party wasn't here. None of her friends has ever scored that much booze for a party before. And usually it's been beer, enough for one each at most, or a mickey of something that everyone gets a sip or two of. It might be fun, though, thinks Kennedy, to see Jordan a little tipsy. Maybe that's what it'll take to loosen him up.

"Music. We need music to clean by," says Sarina before taking a second gulping drink.

"Kennedy?" comes her father's voice on his way downstairs.

"Yeah, Dad?" She gestures to Sarina to hide the bottle.

Sarina quickly screws the top back on and stuffs it in the closet. Home late from work tonight, Dad had missed dinner. Again.

"Your mom said you were having some friends over, so I picked up some chips and pop on my way home," he says, coming round the corner. He places two large bags of chips and a case of root beer on Kennedy's desk. Dad never buys Coke or Pepsi because of the caffeine. At least it isn't Five-Alive, thinks Kennedy, like last time.

Her father's tall, six-foot-three, lean but not gawky thin. Kennedy takes after his side of the family. His sister, Kennedy's Aunt Cathy, is a slender five-ten. Already five-nine and three-quarters, Kennedy is counting on growing one quarter inch taller and absolutely no more.

"Thanks, Dad."

"Yeah, thanks, Mr. Baines," echoes Sarina, the smile on her face a little too happy.

Kennedy can smell the booze on Sarina's breath and prays Dad can't.

"You're welcome," he says and turns to go. "Big party tonight?"

"Just a few friends."

He nods and turns to leave. He's so trusting, thinks Kennedy, suddenly wanting to throw her arms around him, tell him about her day. She doesn't, though, because Sarina would think she's insane.

Kennedy's dad is older than her mom, twelve years older, in fact, but still Kennedy thinks of her parents as perfect complements — like fire and wood. Her dad's a marine biologist, "a fish doctor," as Liam calls him, and has a slow, mannered style that makes it easy to picture him in an ascot and vest, a long "Mr. Darcy" coat. She secretly likes that he insists on proper sit-down dinners and makes her and Liam write thank-you notes to the relatives after birthdays and Christmas.

Dad's a reader, like her. He bought her all sorts of books when she was little, like *Miss Rumphius* and *The*

Balloon Tree. Those books, and others, are now officially Tory's, who'll probably colour all over them or cut out all the "kitties" from the pictures. And like Kennedy, Dad has trouble making decisions. Mom's the decision-maker — though since she's so impulsive, they're not always good ones — like how she painted the living room walls three times before she found a colour she liked or ... Kennedy pictures her mom kissing that director and blinks the image away.

Her dad's grey head disappears around the corner and Kennedy feels an inexplicable sense of loss. He's gone totally grey this past year, which she finds depressing. When Dad takes Tory to the playground, people ask if she's his granddaughter. Kennedy's even been asked, more than once, if Tory was hers. Her daughter? Right. It was weird to her that those people thought she'd had sex. Did she look as if she had? Kennedy thought she could pick out which girls at school had lost their virginity. A certain carefree quality was gone from their eyes and their movements were heavier, more deliberate, as if sex carried with it some sort of weight.

"Let's get cleaning," sings Sarina as Billie Joe Armstrong's sexy tenor erupts from the speakers. "But first," she reaches into the closet, "one more sip."

"Slow down, Sarina. The party's not for another hour."

Sarina doesn't seem to hear her. There's a recklessness about Sarina tonight that Kennedy doesn't recognize.

4

Jordan and Chase are the first to arrive. Luckily the downstairs has its own entrance off the carport so nobody has to ring the front doorbell and be subject to Dad's scrutiny or Mom's chumminess. Jordan's wearing new khakis that hang low on his hips and drag lightly on the ground. Nice. And he's got on his black ribbed T-shirt that fits his body like a glove. He stands shyly in the doorway and says hi with a limp wave of his hand while Chase walks right in to "change this girl music."

"It is not," says Sarina. She punches his arm and Chase smiles.

Determined tonight will be different, Kennedy goes and hugs Jordan hello. She wishes he'd just kiss her, long and luscious, right here and now. She removes her arms and he crosses his over his chest, his cute face flushing pink. Kennedy turns away, disappointed, and asks Sarina for a swig of that rum, hoping Jordan gets the message.

Graham and Willow arrive hand in hand, Amber flanking Willow's other side like a faithful dog. Willow's wearing skintight turquoise jeans and a skimpy halter top that shows her ample cleavage. Amber, who's three sizes big-ger than Willow — with the exception of her bra size — and self-conscious about her weight, is in her usual uni-form of jeans and a bag of a sweatshirt. Willow looks "in a mood," her eyes impatient, her mouth puckered into a pout. Graham, who's at least a year older than anybody else because he had to repeat grade six, is wearing a red muscle shirt to show off his scabby new tattoo not to mention the pimples ringing his neck. Graham gives Kennedy the creeps. She really can't understand Willow's taste in guys.

"Hi, everyone, we're here," says Amber, as if speaking for all three of them. She heads for the bowl of potato chips.

Miko is dropped off by her mom, who looks identical to Miko — full-moon faces with shoulder-length black hair and narrow smiles. Kennedy imagines Miko looks exactly the same now as she did at two, only bigger, and will look the same at sixty, only greyer. Terminally late, Brice announces his 8:30 arrival by letting off a Screecheroo in the road in front of the house. Everyone heads outside as he lights up another and Kennedy sees Dad standing at the living room window looking concerned. She smiles and waves and he lifts a hand in return. Chase's music choice, Red Hot Chili Peppers, seems to have magically gotten louder and Kennedy goes inside to turn it down. Someone has flicked the TV to Much Music and Avril Lavigne clashes rhythms with the Peppers' "Other Side."

Back outside, Brice starts a game of horse with the bas-ketball. Chase and Jordan join him. Kennedy would play too, but Miko hates sports so Kennedy sits beside her on the grass to watch instead. Besides, she likes watching

Jordan move. He's smooth and athletic, thin but muscled too. And he's aggressive on the court. She can tell he's trying harder because she's watching. When he ends up winning, he catches Kennedy's eye with a shy but proud smile. She smiles back.

Inside, Sarina holds the twix in one hand and a can of pop in the other. "Rum and root beer?" she offers.

"Holy shit," says Brice, staring at the rum. "Where'd you get that?"

"Granny," says Sarina sweetly, then proceeds to chug the Bacardi straight out of the bottle.

"You'll germ it," snarls Graham, who pops open a root beer, sips some off and refills it with the rum.

Kennedy follows suit and offers to make one for Jordan.

"No, thanks," he says politely, as if speaking to an adult.

"Fine," she says, annoyed. What does "being a couple" mean, she thinks, if he's immobilized by shyness? She'll have to drink enough for both of them.

"Quit touching me," Willow barks at Graham beside her on the couch. She stands up, adjusts her halter top and storms outside.

Graham gives her the finger and knocks back his root beer. Amber trots after her friend, shooting Graham a look over her shoulder that he doesn't even notice. He grabs the channel changer, flicks to the wrestling channel, then slumps back on the couch with a grunt.

"What's with Willow?" asks Kennedy as Amber hustles past.

"Graham was talking up the girl at Video Stop, you know the one with the dreads?"

"Who has the stray eye?"

Amber nods. "So Willow's pissed," she whispers. "I better catch up with her."

Kennedy takes her drink over to Jordan. "Come on, one sip," she says and holds it up to his lips.

He snickers and allows her to tip some into his mouth. His skin's noticeably clearer tonight, she thinks, watching as root beer trickles down the side of his mouth. She catches it up with a slow finger and their eyes meet. She brushes his lips ever so slightly, easing the drip into his mouth. She's the one who's blushing now, and quickly takes another drink.

"Slow it down," Chase is saying to Sarina and he tries to wrestle the rum bottle away from her. Chase, who's had a crush on Sarina since the third grade, is always looking out for her. Sarina's only ever liked Chase as a friend, but Kennedy can tell he's never stopped hoping.

"I'm not drunk," Sarina insists, coughing out a laugh. "You are."

She wrenches the bottle free and stumbles backward to hit the wall, knocking a painting off its nail — a landscape Kennedy painted in grade seven that Mom had insisted on framing.

"Oh, shit. Sorry, Kennedy," says Sarina, her hand springing up to cover her mouth. "I'll buy you another," she says, reaching for Kennedy's shoulder. "Don't be mad at me."

"Nothing's broken," says Kennedy, tucking the picture behind the couch where it belongs.

"All fixey?" says Sarina, grinning.

"You're talking like a three-year-old, Sarina."

"I'm tall for a three-year-old." Her eyes widen.

Kennedy laughs. "Just don't start calling me Kendy."

"No, no, never," she promises, making a wavy cross over her heart.

"Did you eat anything before you came over?" asks Kennedy. Sarina seems awfully drunk, awfully fast.

"Maybe not," says Sarina, leaning a heavy head against Kennedy's arm. "Wanted a flat stomach." She pats her inverted stomach and Kennedy shakes her head.

"As if you need to worry." There's nothing large about Sarina, in any direction.

"Come on, Sarina," says Chase, putting his hand around her waist. "I'll take you outside for some air." He slips the bottle out of Sarina's hands and quickly passes it to Kennedy, gesturing with his eyes for her to hide it.

"Just slap her a few times," says Graham. "She'll sober up."

"Not nice," says Sarina, pointing at Graham with an unsteady finger.

Chase takes Sarina outside and Kennedy tucks the bottle behind the couch next to her painting. Jordan is tossing darts on the dart board in the corner. She takes a long sip of her rum and root beer and walks up behind him. Slipping an arm around his waist, she crooks her head toward her bedroom, knowing he'd never kiss her in front of other people. "Come with me."

He smiles shyly but puts down the darts.

Unfortunately, when they step into Kennedy's room, Miko is lying on her floor flipping through a magazine and Brice is putting a new CD on the stereo. Kennedy sighs and sits on the bed, pulling Jordan down beside her. Brice and Miko won't stay in here forever, she figures, running a hand down Jordan's back.

Brice starts talking about how he's making fifteen dollars an hour doing some landscape work for his mother's new boyfriend. "All I have to do is mow lawns and pull a few weeds. It's all right."

"Fifteen an hour? That's more than my mom makes," says Miko.

"What's minimum now? Six?"

"Yeah, used to be eight until the Liberals got in power."

"I applied for part-time work at Bolen Books and at that little bookstore down in Cadboro Bay," says Kennedy, "but neither store is hiring right now. Bolen's said to try again in September. I think they still pay eight."

She catches a faint smell of paint through the open window, hears voices in the backyard. She cranes her neck to see outside, forgetting that the view of the yard is now blocked by the half dozen hydrangeas Mom planted last fall. She sips her rum and root beer.

"Bolen's would be the perfect place for you, Kennedy." says Miko. "Sarina's lucky, getting that job at The Gap."

"She got that job because she buys so much stuff there," laughs Kennedy.

"Nice to have rich parents," mumbles Brice.

"It's her mom," says Kennedy. "She's some big curator person for the museum. Her dad's a swim coach."

"Where *is* Sarina?" asks Miko.

"Chase took her outside to sober up."

"She seems pretty hammered. Somebody should cut her off," says Brice.

"We got the bottle away from her," says Kennedy. "God, I just hope my parents don't see her." A buzzy warmth is suddenly weighting her chest and arms: the effects of the rum. She can feel herself relaxing. She runs a hand down Jordan's thigh.

Suddenly Jordan's hand is stroking her neck, a tentative tickle but it sends delicious shivers over Kennedy's scalp. Closing her eyes, she turns him into Colin Firth in white riding breeches and a brown knee-length coat. She sends Miko and Brice a telepathic message to leave.

"What's that smell?" asks Brice.

"Is it paint?" says Miko.

"Yeah," Kennedy says, reluctantly opening her eyes. "I smelled it a minute ago. You guys should go see what —"

A breathless Amber bursts through the door. "Come quick, Sarina's ..." she hesitates, "had an accident."

Kennedy's up in an instant, hurrying after Amber to the bathroom she cleaned this afternoon. Sarina is sitting on the closed toilet, smiling sweetly, her jean capris stained a darker blue all down the crotch and inner thighs. Yellow liquid is dripping off the toilet seat onto the floor.

"I went pee," Sarina sings and proceeds to fall, head first, onto the floor before anyone can catch her. She rolls onto her back, kicking her wet legs in the air, oblivious to the fresh cut on her forehead and the blood running into one eye.

She's hit the corner of the baseboard heater, thinks Kennedy, kneeling beside her friend to make sure she doesn't hurt herself again.

Everyone's crowded into the bathroom doorway now.

"She's cut herself," Miko says in a squeamish voice.

"She's out of it," says Brice.

"Could be alcohol poisoning," Graham says authoritatively. "You pee your pants if you've got alcohol poisoning."

"She peed?" Willow sounds revolted.

"Is she going to die?" whimpers Miko.

"Die?" repeats Sarina, kicking her legs gleefully.

"You better get your mom, Kennedy," says Chase. "What if Graham's right?"

"And she might need stitches for that cut," says Amber.

"Okay," says Kennedy, wishing this wasn't happening. "Don't let her get up," she tells Chase, "in case she falls again."

Kennedy rushes upstairs, wondering if her breath smells of rum. God, what if Sarina is seriously sick? That would be awful. And would Kennedy's parents be legally responsible? She didn't know Sarina was bringing booze. Really she didn't. Why did she agree to have the party here? Dad is going to be so upset if he finds out.

Kennedy's father is in the living room watching baseball. Act calm, nonchalant, she tells herself. Liam's watching the game too. Obviously bored, he's bouncing his head on the back of his chair, listing off oxymorons. She doesn't know how Dad can stand to let Liam go on like he does.

"Pure poison, jumbo shrimp, black light, military intelligence, pretty ugly, straight angle, boneless ribs —"

"Where's Mom?" Kennedy interrupts, sounding as casual as she can.

"Reading to Tory," says Dad. "Everything okay?" He glances past her down the stairs.

"Oh, great," she says, then adds, "it's just ... girl stuff." Girl stuff is her and Mom's euphemism for anything related to menstruation. This always stops his questioning cold.

"Mmm," says Dad, looking back to the TV.

She hurries down the hall and quietly opens the door to her old room.

"I hate to interrupt, Mom, but we've had an incident."

"Incident?"

"In-ci-denk," repeats Tory. A gallery of stuffed animals lines the wall behind her, half of them Kennedy's old stuffies. She's snuggling what was Kennedy's favourite, a cheetah named Cheerio, which Tory has renamed Fire for some logic-less reason.

"Just, you have to come," Kennedy pleads with urgent jerks of her head. "Now, please."

"I'll get Daddy to finish the book, Tory, then I'll come back and kiss you goodnight."

"Hurry," says Kennedy under her breath. She fills her mom in on the way downstairs. "I'm so sorry, Sarina drank a bunch of her grandmother's rum and fell —" Her mother stops listening and pushes past.

"She's messed," says Brice, as people part to let Kennedy's mom into the bathroom.

"I want to dance," Sarina is saying, pumping her arms in the air.

"We think she forgot to pull down her pants. We found her sitting on the toilet all wet, then she fell and cut herself on the heater," Kennedy explains. "Could she have alcohol poisoning?"

"Alcohol poisoning? God, how much did she drink?"

"I don't know," says Kennedy.

"A lot," says Chase. "A quarter or maybe a third of a twix?"

"What's a twix?"

"A twenty-sixer."

Mom shakes her head. "Sarina, look at me."

Sarina looks at Kennedy's mom and smiles. "Hi cool mom who's home," she slurs.

"She's making eye contact and knows who I am,"

says Mom. "Those are good signs. Miko, help me get her out of these pants and Kennedy, go get a pair of your sweatpants. Are there any Band-Aids down here?"

"Under the sink."

"And Kennedy," adds her mom, "shut the door behind you."

Kennedy does as she's told. Chase follows her into her bedroom, asking if there's anything he can do. His face looks pained, as if he's blaming himself.

"No, I don't think so. She should be okay." She squeezes his arm, to reassure him. "It's not your fault."

Despite Sarina's "dancing," Kennedy's mom manages to dress the cut, pinning the two sides together with a butterfly bandage.

"Do you think she'll need stitches?" asks Miko.

"No, it's not deep — just a bleeder."

The three of them peel off Sarina's wet pants and underwear, then work her legs into a pair of Kennedy's way-too-long sweatpants and roll up the cuffs. With Kennedy on one side and Miko on the other, they guide Sarina to the bedroom and into Kennedy's bed. A few minutes later, Mom brings down a bottle of water and two pieces of bread. "To dilute the alcohol in her system," she says.

"Mom? I'm really sorry about this," Kennedy says, watching her mom gently stuff a balled-up piece of bread between Sarina's smiling lips. "Are you mad?"

"Eat up, Sarina. Come on," Mom urges. "I'm not mad. We've all gotten plastered in our time."

It's times like this that Kennedy's grateful for having a mother like hers. Anybody else's mom would be freaking out. Miko's parents would have called an ambulance and the police by now.

"Just don't tell your father," Mom's quick to add.

I've kept secrets from him before, Kennedy thinks, and suddenly notices that Mom's shirt is unbuttoned down to her bra.

"Mom," Kennedy says, pointing to her shirt.

"Oh," laughs Mom, doing up one button. Two would have been better, thinks Kennedy.

"Are you going to call her folks?" asks one of the heads now peering around the bedroom doorway.

"Why?" says Mom and the others murmur their approval. "We'll keep an eye on her for now. She should be all right come morning, besides having the world's worst headache."

Kennedy hopes people don't think hers is the no-limits house after this. All she needs now is that bowl of condoms in the bathroom.

"But if there's more alcohol down here, I want it now," says Mom, much to Kennedy's relief.

"Can you get it, Chase?" says Kennedy. "I stashed it behind the couch."

Chase comes in a minute later with the bottle.

"Jamaican rum," says Mom, making a sour face. "Well, you, Kennedy, have to make sure Sarina doesn't get out of this bed. Keep feeding her bread and water and keep her turned on her side, in case she ..." Mom opens her mouth and gestures with her hand. "Which would be a good thing, actually. To get it out of her system. I'll fetch a bucket."

As her mom urges the other kids to go about their business and let Sarina sleep it off, Jordan slips into the bedroom.

"Want to babysit with me?" asks Kennedy.

"Sure."

Sarina's eyes have closed. For a moment, lying so still, it does look as if she's fallen asleep. Kennedy is about to ask Jordan to sit down, when Sarina hurls herself up to sitting, her eyes springing open.

"Whoa," says Kennedy, looking at Jordan. Together they push Sarina back down. Sarina instantly closes her eyes and lies still again.

"That reminded me of that zombie movie we saw at Amber's," says Jordan. "Where the girl pops out of the coffin?"

"Yeah, that was so creepy."

Mom opens the door and comes in carrying an empty ice cream container. "Are you feeding her bread and water?" She stops, smiles when she sees Jordan. "Hi, Jordan."

"Hi, Mrs. Baines," he says, looking to the floor.

Kennedy quickly breaks off a piece of bread and urges Sarina to eat.

"And try wrapping her up in the blankets," says Mom, placing the bucket on the floor beside the bed. "Swaddling her should help keep her on her side. I'll come check on her after a little while."

"Are you sure she doesn't have to go to the hospital?" asks Kennedy, suddenly questioning her mom's judgement.

"I've seen much worse," says her mom with a snicker.

How reassuring. Mom leaves, shutting the bedroom door behind her. Kennedy sighs. Left in charge again.

She shoots Jordan an apologetic smile. If the party hadn't been at her house, this wouldn't be happening.

PAIN #8: RESPONSIBILITY

"Sorry, I guess we're stuck in here."

Jordan smiles back sheepishly. "That's okay."

He's so sweet, thinks Kennedy, moving over to make room for him on the bed.

"So, are you going anywhere this summer?"

"We go to Parksville pretty soon for a couple weeks. You?"

"No, my dad has to work all summer."

"Oh, yeah."

The sudden silence is fat with self-consciousness.

"Oh, Sarina," sighs Kennedy, "why did you drink that much?"

As if in answer, Sarina pops up to sitting again. "Let's dance," she slurs, trying to get up off the bed. Kennedy tackles her back down.

"Help me wrap her up," she says to Jordan. "Tight."

Using Kennedy's comforter and extra blanket, they swaddle her like a giant baby. Sarina struggles happily. "You gooda, gooda guys," she says.

"What does that mean?" Kennedy laughs, and Jordan shrugs, laughing now too.

"Two houses," Sarina says, shaking her head.

"Sounds like Shakespeare," says Kennedy, and Jordan looks at her blankly. Kennedy's second-favourite movie of all time is *Shakespeare in Love*, which also has Colin Firth in it.

She feeds Sarina some water, which Sarina spews forth like a whale.

"Sarina, don't," scolds Kennedy.

"Don't," repeats Sarina. Then her eyes roll back in her head and show white. Kennedy shudders.

"You have to drink some water, now, come on." Kennedy lifts her friend's head forward and wets her lips with the water.

Sarina's eyes refocus and she drinks a little, then eats another bread ball. Her eyes shut again. Sitting on the ends of the blankets so they don't unravel, Kennedy and Jordan wait for Sarina's next move.

A few minutes pass. "She seems to be really asleep this time," says Kennedy.

"Passed out is more like it."

"Yeah. She started drinking when she came over to help me clean."

After another awkward silence, Kennedy gets up to put on music. Knowing that Jordan won't complain, she puts Green Day back on. Then she sits back down beside him, hip to hip. To her surprise he leans over and slips his face under her hair.

"Mmm," comes out of her mouth before she can stop it.

Then she feels his lips suctioning onto her neck. A hickey? He's giving me a hickey? Hickeys are grade eight, grade seven even. She's beyond hickeys, she thinks, but doesn't pull away. It's a start, she tells herself, and shifts her body until her left breast presses against his side. She feels him tense at first, then he gently pushes back. All right. She lets her head fall to the side, to give his mouth more room. The suction hurts slightly and she wonders if the person who invented the hickey was a sadist.

"Stay!" yells Sarina, bolting upright, flailing and kicking at her blanket cocoon.

"Oh shit," says Kennedy, pulling free of Jordan's suction. His clinging lips release with a pop.

"Jordan, help," she orders. Sarina thrashes, trying to get free of the blankets, and her hand accidentally slaps Kennedy's face, hard.

"Hey, that hurt." Kennedy's cheek burns along with the spot on her neck.

Together she and Jordan hold Sarina down and retighten the blankets. Jordan is breathing hard, as if he's lost air giving her the hickey. "She's strong for her size," he grunts.

"Keep her down, I'm going to go look for some rope," says Kennedy. But before she gets up, she leans over a squirming, growling Sarina and gives Jordan a quick but forceful kiss. Focused on a struggling Sarina, Jordan has his mouth partially open and she ends up kissing more teeth than anything.

Stepping into the rec room, Kennedy wipes Jordan's spittle from her lips. The next one will be a real kiss, she tells herself. They just have to get Sarina back to sleep. Maybe she could even encourage his hands to do some exploring. If only he'd planted a hickey on her hip. Now that could have been cool, romantic even, and something to show Sarina and Miko later. She hurries to hunt down the rope she's seen in the rec room closet.

Apparently the party's continued without her. MuchMusic is playing rap music, which Kennedy hates; Willow and Graham are making up, read making out, on the couch, his hand wedged down the back of her jeans; Amber's trying to sort out some impossible brain-teaser toy of Liam's; and Miko is putting tiny braids in Brice's hair while arguing with Chase about masturbation. Nobody seems to notice Kennedy rummaging in the closet for rope.

"It's gross," says Miko. "Besides, I have long nails."

"It's not gross," argues Chase. "It's normal."

"Maybe for guys."

Willow and Graham laugh up close to each other's faces, sharing a private joke. Kennedy hears the rec room door open and sees her mom enter with a cup of what smells like coffee, presumably for Sarina.

"I don't masturbate and never will," says Miko. "It's disgusting."

"What?" says Kennedy's mom.

Kennedy's stomach shrink-wraps.

"Mom," she calls from inside the closet, but it's too late.

"If a woman doesn't learn how to pleasure herself, she'll have an awfully hard time receiving pleasure from her partner," Mom begins.

"No, please," mumbles Kennedy.

PAIN #9: UNSOLICITED PARENTAL ADVICE

She stops her rope search to assess the damage. Chase is smiling in disbelief but nodding, as if in approval. A dumbstruck Miko looks horrified and Brice is confused. Amber mouths the word "gross" and gets up to go to the chip bowl. Willow isn't listening, but Graham's lips have peeled back into a snarl.

"Mom," Kennedy says more loudly, "is that coffee for Sarina?"

"Really, Miko, masturbation, alone or with your partner, is perhaps the best form of birth control you kids could —"

"Mom, in here now, please," Kennedy nearly yells, abandoning her rope search.

"Right on, Mrs. Baines," says Chase, and the whole room starts laughing.

"Sorry, Kennedy," her mother whispers as Kennedy guides her to the bedroom, "but what a thing to say. I always pictured Japanese women liberated in matters of —"

"Help!" comes a forlorn cry from Kennedy's room.

The pungent reek of vomit hits Kennedy's nose first. Then she sees Jordan sitting on the bed, his arms held up in surrender. He's looking down at his new khakis, now camouflaged in puke, while Sarina sits upright in her clean Gap T-shirt, grinning, her head weaving soft figure eights.

"She's going to be fine," says Mom.

After her purge, Sarina passes out for good, snoring sweetly. Jordan goes home to change but doesn't come back. A subdued party continues until eleven-thirty, when, after knocking first, Dad sticks his head in and politely but firmly asks everyone who isn't sleeping over to leave. After people have left, Kennedy and Miko watch a movie, complain in the dark about all the hot guys being in grade twelve, and drop off to sleep a little after two. It's still dark when Kennedy wakes to someone talking.

"I have terrible cramps. Can you please pick me up?"

Kennedy opens one sleepy eye to see Sarina talking into her cell phone. In a haze, she watches her pale-faced friend quietly gather her things and tiptoe out of the room, closing the door behind her as soundlessly as she can. Then Kennedy drifts back to sleep.

"Kennedy! Kennedy!"

In her dream, someone is calling her name, someone's in trouble. Graham is giving her a hickey, around her belly button. It isn't a good feeling, but he is going to kiss her soon and is turning into Ryan Slaters in grade twelve, the hunky school president, which makes it all right.

"Kennedy!" she hears again and is reluctantly pulled awake.

It's more of an angry yell than a call for help, she thinks now. And not a nice way to wake up.

"Who's yelling?" groans Miko.

"I think it's my mom," says Kennedy. "Go back to sleep." She gets up before the yelling wakes Sarina too. No, Sarina left, didn't she? Kennedy looks at the cat sleeping in the jumble of covers on her empty bed.

"Kennedy!" she hears again. Sounds like it's coming from the backyard. God, what could have happened? Mom sounds furious. She grabs her glasses and makes her way outside, still in her pyjamas. The grass is a cool, damp carpet under her feet.

Tory is jumping on the trampoline, naked except for a pair of red shorts. Every exposed area of her skin is lined with blue marker. In between the lines are the faded pink spots of her chicken pox.

"Look at me, Kendy, I'm a cougar." She does a turning jump and scratches her hands in the air.

"Cougars don't have stripes," says Kennedy.

"Yes, they do." Tory jumps forward and swipes at her sister with a clawed hand.

Her mom is standing over by their upturned yellow canoe, frowning. She's holding something in her hand, a can of some kind.

"Mom, what is it?"

"Come see for yourself."

Coming closer, Kennedy sees Mom's holding a can of what looks like spray paint. *Fuck Bin Ladin* is written in sloppy black letters from one end of the canoe to the other. For a second she wonders why her mother would do such a thing, then flashes on the smell of paint last night. Oh shit. Graham?

"And who do you suppose is the artist?" asks Mom.

"Mom, I have no idea, truly," Kennedy says. "Some stupid person, though."

"Well, it had to be one of *your* friends, so it'll be *your* responsibility to clean it up."

There's that r-word again. Kennedy feels the beginning of a headache behind her right eye.

"Sure Mom, I'll do it."

Mom looks at the canoe and shakes her head. "'Laden' is not spelled with an 'i'."

Typical that Mom would care more about a misspelled

word on her canoe than the f-word.

"I'll have to go to Canadian Tire and find out what takes this paint off," says Mom, sighing. "So is our Sarina alive and kicking this morning?"

"She left early. Called her parents."

"I want you to call and check up on her. Hopefully her parents won't sue us." Mom doesn't sound nearly as cavalier as she did last night.

"Kendy, look what I can do," calls Tory again.

Kennedy looks over as her striped sister does a crumpled cartwheel. Kennedy claps three times instead of speaking. It takes less energy.

"Is that a bug bite on your neck?" Mom reaches her hand out and Kennedy quickly scratches the spot and fingers her hair forward to cover it.

"Yeah, I think the cat has fleas."

Kennedy heads directly to the bathroom to check out Jordan's handiwork in the mirror. A perfect football shape in gradations of purple. She groans, then pats at her frizzed-out hair. She tries to imagine Mr. Darcy giving Elizabeth Bennet a hickey. Impossible.

Dad makes blueberry crepes for breakfast, and Miko is gone by eleven. Kennedy locates some rubber gloves and goes outside to sweat under the sun while spraying vaporous poison onto the canoe. The spray makes her light-headed and she imagines thousands more brain cells going belly-up beside the rummed ones, her IQ rapidly declining.

"It would have been easier to spray the whole thing black," says Liam, suddenly behind her.

She turns and glares at him. His eyebrows look even whiter and weirder today, the freckles on his nose almost a solid blanket of brown.

"A black canoe would be cool," he says, erroneously continuing to speak. "The Black Mission, we could call it. Or the Dark Blade. Or Night Row."

"Go away unless you're going to help," says Kennedy. Her arm is already aching.

"Sorry, Kennedy, but I gotta go put my feet up, have a cold drink, eat some gourmet chips and dip —"

"Go!" she yells.

After Liam's gone, Kennedy twists her hair up into a knot to get it off her neck. Stretching her aching back, she stares up at the clouds. She loves watching clouds and how they're always changing shape, however slowly and imperceptibly. She hears Tory over in the tree house, talking to herself, lost in some make-believe world, and is suddenly filled with envy. Sometimes it seems like only last week when she was the one riding on Dad's shoulders, above it all, or carried half asleep in his arms as if she weighed next to nothing. Kennedy can still remember the elaborate lives she made up for each of her Barbies. Lives without consequences, without real concerns. Now life seems so ... so dire.

"Better start career planning," say the teachers at school.

"You should start doing your own wash," says Mom. "You're old enough now and I have enough housework."

"The Fisheries are hiring kids to clean up beaches this summer," her dad announced the other night.

PAIN #10: GROWING UP

She doesn't want to think about what she wants to be. She doesn't want to spend her summer picking up people's garbage. She wants to sleep in, read books, laze on the beach with friends. She wants her mom to do her laundry for her, her dad to check in on her before she goes to sleep.

The clouds shift and the sudden glaring sun makes her look away. She sprays more paint remover on the canoe and starts rubbing.

The thought of turning into an adult, "a dolt" as Liam would say, is frightening. Adults seem to have dropped the word "fun" from their vocabulary. And the word "happy." Their lives are so plugged with responsibilities and complicated with "issues." Everything she reads in the paper or hears on the news is totally depressing, and adults are responsible for it.

The only time any of the adults she knows come close to being happy is if they've been drinking or are stoked up on pharmaceuticals like Mrs. Hartford, her science teacher. Mrs. Hartford laughs at everything, sometimes until tears run down her face. She assigns homework, then forgets all about it. Everyone says that since Mrs. Hartford's husband left, she's been on "happy pills." But she doesn't seem happy, only manically sad. Then there's scary Mr. Larkin, their gung-ho art teacher, who, rumour has it, smokes dope for breakfast. He plays the freakiest music in class — like that Tibetan thigh-bone music with the overtone singing — and sees meaning in the simplest of drawings. Even her own parents — who she'd term well adjusted — seem to need a couple of drinks to remember how to laugh. Being an adult looks miserable.

Now even most of Kennedy's friends seem bent on drinking when they can, though Sarina takes the cake for getting the most drunk ever. Pot will be next, thinks Kennedy. Graham already smokes and Willow's done it a few times. Of course, Willow will try anything.

"A good rule for drugs," Mom told Kennedy once, during a commercial showing how marijuana reduced kids to forgetful retards, "is to just do half of what everyone else does."

An insidious invitation, Kennedy thought at the time, to join the ranks of depressed adults who need stimulants to enjoy anything.

An hour later, the letters of "*Fuck*" have faded but certainly haven't disappeared. It looks as if they've only been absorbed deeper into the fibreglass. Kennedy is spraying the "*L*" of "*Ladin*" when her dad comes around the corner in his cuffed shorts and golf shirt. He's wearing his new runners, beige with white soles, that resemble skateboarders' shoes. They must have been on sale at Sears. On the ends of Dad's long pale legs, and with black socks no less, the skater shoes look a lot less than cool.

"Need a hand?" he asks, and Kennedy can't help but sigh.

"My arm's killing me. Thanks, Dad."

"Didn't ask if you needed an arm." They snicker together. "I feel a little responsible for leaving that can of spray paint out," says Dad. "I used it for a scratch on the van door and forgot to put it away."

He takes the can of cleaner and starts spraying the "*B*" of "*Bin.*"

"This smells awful," he says, and Kennedy nods.

"We might start talking like Liam after breathing this stuff," she says.

Dad catches her eye and they both laugh out loud.

Kennedy smiles to herself. It's nice to be alone with her dad for a change. Back in Fredericton, before Tory came along, she and Dad used to play cards together, go for nature hikes and long quiet rides on the St. John River in this very canoe. Any free time he has now, he spends reading to Tory or playing squash with Liam. As if he thinks she's too old for his attention, wouldn't want it. They scrub on in happy silence. Kennedy loves her dad more than anyone. Parents say they love all their kids equally but it's only because they have to say that. It's not any truer than a child loving both parents equally. She's always felt that Mom connects more easily to Liam, just as Kennedy connects more easily to Dad. It's just the way it is. Biology. Yet since Tory came along, "the baby of the family" and another girl, things are no longer so clear-cut.

"Great that Mom's taking up acting again, eh?" says Dad.

"Yeah, great." Kennedy suddenly remembers her hickey and with her free hand pulls her hair out of its knot to cover her neck.

"Don't you miss going to see her plays?"

"Not really."

The job's finally done, despite the letters' ghostly remains. Kennedy calls to check on Sarina but nobody answers. She makes herself some lunch and escapes into *Pride and Prejudice*. Elizabeth is just about to meet Mr. Wickham at a party that's taking place at her Aunt Philips'. Wickham is a member of the regiment now stationed in Meryton and, as Elizabeth is soon to find out, a boyhood friend of Mr. Darcy's.

Mr. Wickham was the happy man towards whom almost every female eye was turned, and Elizabeth was the happy woman by whom he finally seated himself; and the agreeable manner in which he immediately fell into conversation, though it was only on its being a wet night, and on the probability of a rainy season, made her feel that the commonest, dullest, most threadbare topic might be rendered interesting by the skill of the speaker.

He speaks eagerly of his past dealings with Mr. Darcy, whom, not to Elizabeth's surprise, Wickham accuses of having cheated him out of the living that his godfather, Mr. Darcy's late father, had bequeathed upon him — hence his present impoverished position in society.

Even the wicked men were charming back then, thinks Kennedy, biting into her sandwich.

On Wednesday, Dad announces at dinner that

Mom has something to share with everybody.

"I got a call from the theatre today and I'm in," she says, holding her hands in the air.

"Winner!" says Liam. He holds up three fingers to make a "w" which he places behind Tory's head.

"Mommy wins," screeches Tory.

Dad lifts his glass of wine to raise a toast and everyone follows suit, lifting wine and water respectively. All except Kennedy.

"Kennedy, we're congratulating your mom," says Dad.

"I just don't know if it's a great idea," she ventures.

"Kennedy, what do you mean?" Mom says with an airy laugh. Or is it a nervous laugh?

"I mean ..." Kennedy hasn't thought it through, "Tory's not in school yet and Dad's sometimes out of town. I don't want to be the one in charge around here."

"It's just one play, Kennedy. A month or so of rehearsals and a week of shows. It'll be over by the time school starts.

And don't worry, I'll hire a sitter if you and Liam are busy."

Kennedy holds her mother's gaze. "And then there'll be more plays, more time away, more ..." She wants to say directors but can't.

Mom doesn't bat an eye. "Kennedy, relax," she says dismissively, then turns to Liam. "I think you'll like this play, Liam, it's set in cyberspace."

"Kennedy," says Dad in his concerned, keep-everyone-happy voice. "Let's try and support your mom's interests, please."

But what exactly are Mom's interests? Kennedy looks over at Tory, who's patiently waiting to clink her glass with someone. She picks up her glass.

"To your mom," says Dad.

"To Mom," everyone except Kennedy choruses.

When she clinks glasses with Mom, Mom smiles softly. What does that smile mean? If only she could just say it, just ask her: Did you cheat on Dad in Fredericton? If Kennedy knew the answer, then maybe she could do something to prevent it from happening all over again here. She looks around the table at her family, and her heart winces in her chest. Please don't let anything bad happen to us.

PAIN #11: PINWORMS

A week clear of chicken pox and now Tory has a new and even more disgusting disease — pinworms, also known as threadworm which sounds even grosser. Apparently Tory was up all last night with an "itchy bum." Too sick to think about but, as Mom's informed her, it means that the whole house could be infected. And now everyone has to take some caramel-flavoured chalky yellow medicine.

"How much do you weigh?" asks Mom, a bottle of worm medicine in one hand and a plastic measuring syringe in the other.

"A hundred thirty," she says. "Give or take."

"Okay," Mom reads, "it's 2.5 mL or one-half teaspoon per twenty-five pounds, which means you need approximately two and a half teaspoons." She sucks up the yellow liquid in the syringe and squirts it into a glass. Then does it two more times. "There, you can mix it with water or juice. And we'll all have to repeat the process in two weeks."

"You mean this won't kill them?" Kennedy stares at the sickly yellow paste.

"I think it's a precaution in case any of their eggs hatch later."

"Oh god."

"Actually," says Liam, "the pharmacist said this stuff paralyzes them. Picture all these tiny stiff-necked worms." He freezes in spastic agony, changing poses every two seconds.

"And I have to wash all the sheets and towels in hot water," says Mom, "which means Kennedy, you need to wash yours again."

"I just washed them after the sleepover," she complains. "Less than a week ago." She sniffs at the yellow syrup in the bottom of her glass. It smells bad, like rotten bananas.

"Well, there's nobody to blame here," says Mom. "Tory probably picked them up at preschool. Lots of little hands to keep clean."

Kennedy pours grape juice over the medicine and

watches it slowly rise, like smoke, and infiltrate the juice. She holds her nose and starts to drink.

"Little worm hands," says Liam in a sinister voice, "scratching little worm bums, little worm hands, going into little worm mouths, hatching little worm eggs. Around and around and around it goes —"

"That's enough, Liam," says Mom.

Kennedy's stomach threatens to heave but she wills it down.

"Yeah, thanks, Liam," she says after downing her medicine. "I was only in the middle of drinking it."

"I want some more worm juice," sings Tory as she prances into the kitchen. "It tastes like candy."

"What do we have to look forward to next?" says Kennedy. "Lice, scabies, the plague?"

"We went through similar problems with you and Liam," says Mom. "You were a kid once too, remember."

Which makes me what now?

"Scabies," echoes Liam. "Scabie babies, scabie babies with rabies. Babies with rabies under the kitchen tabies. Craybies maybies ..."

Needing to get out of earshot of Liam's mindless spew, Kennedy leaves. She'll throw her sheets and towels in the washer — again, then go online to see what everyone's up to today. Find out when Jordan's leaving for Parksville.

"Kennedy," calls Mom, "I need you to keep the phone line free this morning. I'm expecting a call from the theatre and also my friend Judith is calling from England. She's coming to Victoria."

"And I claim the computer," yells Liam. "Clan match pronto, Tonto."

Great, thinks Kennedy, starting downstairs. Can't call anyone, can't go on the computer.

"Judith and I were roommates at UNB." Mom is now standing at the top of the stairs, her voice veering nostalgic. "God, we had some wild times."

Don't want to know, thinks Kennedy, but stops on the landing to be polite.

"She lived here in Victoria for several years but moved back to England just before we arrived. Too bad. It would have been nice for our paths to cross again."

Mom is talking to herself now but it would feel rude to leave. Kennedy bites her hangnail.

"Judith has lived in Australia and South Africa. Her husband's in government intelligence or diplomatic relations, I've never been clear on what he does exactly. Something pretty highbrow, though. Apparently spending the summer in Canada is a bit of a last-minute decision on Judith's part. I thought maybe her parents weren't well when she called last week, but she says she just wants out of London for the summer."

"Mom ... your point?" says Kennedy, having pulled out her hangnail, which is now bleeding.

"Oh, that she'll be staying with us for a week, maybe longer, and I'm planning to give her Tory's room. I'll put Tory in with me and Daddy. But her son's also coming and he'll need the couch bed in the rec room. Which means he'll share your bathroom. Can you handle that?"

"Can't he sleep with his mom?" asked Kennedy, picturing a fat eight-year-old who picks his nose.

"He's seventeen, or is it eighteen now, so probably not," says Mom.

"Oh." Kennedy perks up. "What's his name?"

"Connor or Conrad. No, that's not it, Colin. Yeah, Colin."

"Colin?" An eighteen-year-old English guy named Colin, with an accent, no doubt, showering in her bathroom and sleeping on the other side of her bedroom wall?

"So you're okay with that? I think they're coming around the end of the month."

"Yeah, sure."

"Thanks, honey."

Back in her room, Kennedy begins stripping the bed. Tall — he's probably at least six foot, with thick hair, longish, curling slightly at his neck à la Colin Firth in *Pride and Prejudice*. Being eighteen, he's past the pimple stage. His skin is perfect, in fact, and he has to shave, every second morning. In *my* bathroom. And he has lips to die for.

She laughs at herself and flops down on her sheet-free bed. Colin. Picking up her book, she opens to the marked page. She's coming up to the part where Elizabeth discovers, through Mr. Darcy's cousin, Colonel Fitzwilliam, that Mr. Darcy is responsible for convincing Mr. Bingley to give up his newly acquired estate in Longbourn, along with his intentions toward Elizabeth's sister Jane. Jane has been anxiously waiting for word from Mr. Bingley.

"... he congratulated himself on having lately saved a friend from the inconveniences of a most imprudent marriage ..."

"Did Mr. Darcy give you his reasons for this interference?"

"I understood that there were some very strong objections against the lady."

Elizabeth is indignant, believing the proud Mr. Darcy has not only mistreated the handsome Mr. Wickham, but deliberately thwarted her dearest sister's chance for happiness. She believes her sister worthy of any gentleman, no matter their differences in rank and society.

Kennedy's thoughts drift to this Colin guy: does he really have an English accent? His family sounds pretty well off, so maybe he's in line to inherit some whopping fortune. Stop it, she tells herself. He could be an obese dwarf for all she knows. Or freakishly tall with a harelip. And has she forgotten that she's going out with someone? Namely Jordan?

Hoping it's Sarina, Kennedy answers the phone. It's a call from the theatre, a strange man on the other end asking for Leslie. Not Mrs. Baines, not Ms. Baines, not even Leslie Baines. Just Leslie.

"I know my *dad's* here," she says pointedly, though it's not true. "Hold on, please, and I'll see if my *mother's* in."

Reluctantly she calls upstairs for her mom to pick up. Hearing her mom's hello, Kennedy puts her hand over the receiver and hangs on the line to listen.

"Leslie, how's it going?" says the man.

"Fine, David, but hold on a sec. Kennedy," she calls downstairs, "hang up the phone, please."

Kennedy hangs up. Then she has to wait a whole forty-five minutes before the call from England comes through and Mom finally calls out that the phone is free. But by then Liam's clan match is over, so she doesn't care.

Liam starts watching TV, some reality show. "You should know, K-Dot," he says as she sits down at the computer, "that somebody's sniping our yap."

"In English, please?" says Kennedy.

"Hacking our chat, tapping our yak lines. A listening snipe."

"A hacker? Who would want to hack into our conversations?" She logs onto MSN.

"A guy sitting at home in a trench coat, if you catch my drift. They're called cyber-stalkers."

"Whatever." Kennedy is getting impatient.

"I've talked to him. And he asked if I had a sister and how old she was."

"You're lying."

"I swear. Ask Sarah, across the street, she talked to him. He asked her if she slept in her own room."

"Really? That's pretty sick."

"Calls himself Zak." Liam's voice deepens. "Zak Smith. Hella obvious fake name. Says he lives here in Victoria too. Could be a neighbour, even."

"Well, don't talk to him. Put a block on."

"Doesn't mean he won't be..." he lowers his voice, "listening."

"Yeah, sure," says Kennedy.

"Fine, ignore me. I'm telling you that it's a twisted world out there, Kennedy Baines. If that is your real name." He laughs a fake, creepy laugh, flicks off the TV and heads downstairs.

Kennedy has tuned Liam out. There's a message from Jordan.

bored. want 2 meet at sev thn get a movie?

Get a Slurpee at 7-Eleven, go to the movie store and sit on our butts in front of the TV on a sunny day like today?

How creative, thinks Kennedy.

maybe, she writes back. *wen do u leave 4 parksville?*

july 16

When was this Colin guy coming? she wonders.

Message from Chase.

k, next time ms. price sez abstinence is the best birth control Im going to say but ms. baines sez its mutual masturbation

lol

Kennedy had hoped that her mother's little speech last Saturday had been magically erased from everyone's memory. Mom had given Kennedy similar earnest little speeches before, in private. These were disturbing enough. She always made it sound as though masturbation was the key to succeeding in life. Kennedy much preferred her grandmother's "finish high school or you're ruined" speech. The few times Kennedy has tried to masturbate, she's felt silly, and therefore never got past a few pleasant rushes. It just seems to her like the sort of thing that takes two.

chase. do u no who spray-painted r canoe?

wasnt me

wasnt the question

i'm no rat

Sarina's online, wanting to go swimming at Arbutus Cove this afternoon and maybe hike up Mount Doug tonight to see the sun set. Far better suggestions than Jordan's. Sarina always thinks of fun things to do.

hi sar, Kennedy writes back. *sounds great, i'll go. time?*

She leans back in her chair, thinking how weird it is that Sarina hasn't said one word about the party last weekend. Kennedy had brought it up the other day, asked if Sarina's parents said anything, and Sarina acted as if she hadn't heard the question.

"You don't have to be embarrassed," Kennedy had said, and then she touched Sarina on the arm. Sarina jerked her arm away, then with a cheery smile on her face asked if Kennedy had seen last night's episode of *The Simpsons*. "You know the one where Homer's speaking in opposites to that doctor?" Her eyes were oddly blank and Kennedy had felt invisible. "You're overreacting," Sarina said, mimicking the cartoon doctor's officious tone. And, in Homer's voice, "maybe you're *under*-reacting,"— Sarina could do a perfect Homer imitation. Then she laughed, though it had been more like forced air than a real laugh. "This session's over," she went on. "This session's *under*. Goodbye. *Bad* bye."

Kennedy knew that episode well because Liam worked it for weeks after it first aired. Sarina had laughed again and Kennedy politely joined in. After that she didn't dare bring it up again. But the next day they'd run into Chase and Brice near Mount Doug Market. Chase jokingly, and not without affection, greeted Sarina as "the puke princess." Brice laughed, then started to run through the events of that night — the chugging, the peeing, the puking — but Sarina's face had closed down, hardened like a mask, and she simply turned and walked into the store.

"She can't talk about it," Kennedy told them before going after Sarina. Nobody brought it up after that. Especially not Sarina. Fun-loving Sarina. The fact that she ignored it so completely scared Kennedy a little. It made her closest friend seem dishonest and therefore distant. Sarina was becoming yet another thing to worry about.

Kennedy packs a ham sandwich and an apple to take to the beach, plus a bag of chips to share. Chocolate, she thinks, I want to bring chocolate. She starts looking in all of her mom's favourite hiding places. Once she found leftover Easter eggs in Mom's underwear drawer. Another time there were chocolate coins in the cupboard above the fridge — leftovers from Tory's birthday party. Sometimes there's Mom and Dad's respective favourites — Coffee Crisp and Snickers — in the back of the freezer. Today these spots yield nothing.

Where else can she look? she wonders, not ready to give up quite yet, her chocolate craving having increased with the hunt. She eyes the collection of decorator tins on top of the kitchen cupboards. Never looked in those before. She pulls over a chair and starts the process of shaking each tin for evidence. One, two, three empties before ... bingo! something shaking in tin four. It's kind of lightweight for chocolate, but could be leftover pieces of something.

Kennedy takes down the ancient-looking blue and gold Gillette tin. Around its side are pictures of a baby

shaving itself. *Begin early*, it says. *Shave yourself*. Weird.
She turns the can around. *No Stropping, No Honing*. Whatever
that means. She twists off the top and looks inside. A zip-
lock baggie of dark green mashed-together leaves stares
back at her. She lifts it out. Tucked in one corner of the bag
is a small rectangular pack that says Zig-Zag on it. Mom's
dope stash? She opens the bag and smells it, just to be
sure. It's a common enough smell up in the park, only this
smells greener. Kennedy knows her mom smokes now and
again — Mom has insinuated as much — but finding the
evidence feels weird.

Only recently did Kennedy figure out that Mom smokes
when Dad's out of town. The house always feels lost and
directionless when Dad's away, like a ship floating at sea.
It's a noise-ridden and messy ship too, since Mom tends to
listen to her bad seventies — or is it eighties? — music,
cranking up the volume and abandoning housekeeping
to the elves. Tory ends up wearing pyjamas all day, and
sit-down dinners and conversation are replaced by *The
Simpsons*. Dinner is anybody's guess: frozen waffles with
whipped cream, nachos and chocolate-chip cookie dough,
oily KFC if they're lucky.

When Kennedy was younger she chalked up Mom's
general lethargy to her missing Dad, and she felt sympa-
thetic, because she missed him too. Then she realized it was
more a case of Mom taking an in-house holiday. Kennedy
can handle the notion that her mother gets high now and
again, but she doesn't want Liam to know. Not yet. Luckily
Dad's never gone for more than two or three days. The day
of his homecoming is designated "cleaning day," and Mom
ropes everyone in to help. It always feels to Kennedy as if

they're scrubbing away the evidence. By the time Dad pulls up in the drive, the house looks like it did when he left and Mom is back, more or less, to her perky efficient self.

Kennedy wonders if Dad even knows that Mom smokes.

PAIN #13: DISHONESTY

Dishonesty is like a coating of grease that won't come off your hands no matter how much you wash them. And it just adds more confusion when life is confusing enough.

Kennedy puts the bag back in the tin, makes sure the lid is on tight and returns it to the top of the cupboard. She doesn't bother to look in the last two cans. Her chocolate craving is gone.

The afternoon is perfect beach weather. Sarina, Miko, Chase and Jordan show, Sarina with a double-sized air mattress and Chase with a plastic bocce ball set. All five of them paddle around on the air mattress and it feels lovely to lie in the heat of the sun, touching, skin to skin. Kennedy and Chase are the only ones willing to brave the cold water and put their heads under. She tries to pull Jordan in but he fends her off, whining that it's too cold. I'll warm you up, she wants to say, but worries how that might sound and doesn't. They have a bocce ball tournament on the sand, which Jordan wins easily. He confesses he belonged to a bowling club when he was younger.

"Bowling club?" mocks Chase. "What sort of loser are you?"

"He's just recently recovered from his childhood," says Miko. "He played the violin too, remember."

Jordan gives Chase a healthy shove but is blushing just the same.

"I love the violin," says Kennedy, coming to his rescue. "I didn't know you played."

"Not anymore," he says. "Not since hockey."

She knew he played hockey and has heard he's really good. The only thing Chase does is hang out at the skateboard park practising tricks. And he's not even particularly good at it. A skater and a jock. It's surprising how well they get along.

"I used to take figure skating," says Sarina and proceeds to perform a single axle in the sand.

Kennedy took years of piano lessons in Fredericton and had lots of informal singing lessons from her aunt, but doesn't offer this information. The truth is she'd like to take more singing lessons someday. One of her favourite things to do, besides reading a good novel, is to take out her keyboard, play and sing along. She's memorized the love songs from *The Titanic* and *Love Actually*, her dad's favourite Beatles song, "Norwegian Wood," and her mom's favourite "Stairway to Heaven" by Led Zeppelin. She keeps the keyboard and sheet music hidden at the back of her closet, so no one will ask her to play.

"Kennedy has a great voice," Sarina says suddenly, as if reading her thoughts.

"No I don't," says Kennedy, blushing.

"I stood in front of you in grade seven choir, so shut up. Mrs. Wade even asked Kennedy to sing a solo for the year-end concert but she wouldn't." Sarina shakes her head. "Tara Stevens, who can't sing her way out of a paper bag, sang it instead."

"Sing us your solo," says Chase.

Kennedy remembers how badly she wanted to say yes to Mrs. Wade, but it was her first year at the school and she was way too shy.

"For your boyfriend. A love song," he teases.

Kennedy hates this level of talk: boys her age are so afraid to be anything but cynical. Cynical is so safe. So nowhere.

"And what can you do, Chase, besides mock other people?" Kennedy shoots back, then worries those words might be too true and therefore hurtful.

"I can do handstands," he says, unfazed, and pops up from the blanket to heave himself up on his hands.

Before long they're all doing them. Cartwheels too, which Sarina can do best, five consecutive, ending off in a roundup. It comes out that she took gymnastics as well.

After they've resettled on their towels, Kennedy asks if anyone has come across a Zak Smith on MSN.

"Zak Smith," repeats Chase. "That's a fake name if I ever heard one."

"I had some guy online the other day who said he was from New Zealand," says Sarina, picking the sand from between her toes. "I don't remember his name, though."

"My brother thinks this Zak guy is some local perv listening in on our conversations. Apparently he's been asking weird questions."

"Can anyone just listen in? Don't you have to be talking to someone?" Sarina looks up from her feet.

"I think there's some software that hackers use," says Jordan.

"Is that what your mom has, Jordan?" sneers Chase. "To spy on you?"

"She wouldn't have a clue how to do that."

"Your mother spies on you?" asks Kennedy.

"She just signed onto MSN at work to see how much time I spent on it."

"Now *that's* weird," says Miko.

"There could be tons of sleazebags online," says Chase, "pretending they're our age and trying to pick up girls."

"Or guys," says Sarina.

"Even more sick," says Jordan, his voice suddenly deeper.

"Remember that guy with no arms who kidnapped some girl our age?" Miko says. "He met her online, then came to her house and talked her into going away with him. They caught him on the ferry, remember?"

"Oh, yeah, he was a thalidomide baby," says Kennedy. "You know that drug they used to give women for morning sickness? The guy had arms but they were all shrunken."

"Like flippers." Chase folds his hands into his armpits and flaps his elbows.

"God, why would she go with him?" Sarina makes a face.

"Yeah. Well, this Zak guy asked Liam if he had an older sister and asked this other girl if she slept in her own room."

"That's warped."

"What's creepy is that he lives in Victoria." He must, thinks Kennedy, or how else would he have known she was tall? She shivers.

"Tell him to fuck off," says Chase, flapping a flipper arm at Sarina's foot.

Sarina smacks his elbow away. "Fuck off," she says.

When the sun has left the beach in shadow, the air off the bay cools quickly and they all head home. Kennedy and Sarina plan to meet after dinner for a walk up Mount Doug to watch the sunset. Miko wants to come but has to ask her parents. Jordan and Chase have "family stuff," but Jordan offers to walk Kennedy home despite his house being in the opposite direction. Kennedy says sure, and then doesn't feel much like talking. And since Jordan isn't one to initiate conversation, the walk is long and quiet. Her thoughts are caught up in what Sarina said about her singing. Is her voice really above average? She had wanted to join the high-school choir, but heard that the teacher, Ms. Corey, was really mean. Besides, none of her friends were joining.

How Kennedy used to love going at Christmas to hear her Aunt Cathy sing in Handel's *Messiah*. Everyone said Kennedy got her height and her hair from Aunt Cathy. So maybe she got her voice too. Her aunt's choir held a spring concert as well, on Mother's Day, but the *Messiah* was Kennedy's favourite. The powerful rise of all those voices seemed to lift her breath right out of her body. She never failed to have flying dreams the night after that concert. God, when was the last time she's flown in her dreams? Not since moving, anyway. Have they really lived here four years already?

As if by accident, Jordan's hand knocks against hers, derailing her train of thought. Their fingers fumble self-consciously before ending up intertwined. She smiles weakly and he glances shyly at the ground. She'd rather he hadn't walked her home. Would prefer to be alone with her thoughts right now. She remembers badgering Aunt Cathy to give her singing lessons. Mrs. Wade wasn't a bad teacher, but it was her aunt who taught her how to relax the root of her tongue and lift her palate, how to open the back of her throat and feel the notes vibrating the hollow cavities of her face as she pushed them forward. Kennedy pictures herself older, her mother's age, and living on a small island — like Bowen Island, which Mom and Dad took them to last summer, with its tiny village and cool little bookstore. Yeah, she'd live in a cottage, nothing fancy, own or manage a bookstore and sing in a local choir. Perform Handel's *Messiah* every Christmas. Is it bad to have such lowly ambitions?

With Jordan's warm hand in hers, Kennedy wonders if she should kiss him when he drops her off. That would be appropriate. A kiss goodbye. A serious kiss goodbye. His tan makes his zits practically invisible. She didn't know he played violin. The violin is romantic and sexy. They could kiss in the carport, outside her door. Her family will inside by now, getting dinner ready.

As soon as her house comes into view, Jordan lets go of her hand as if afraid that her parents will see them. Maybe he'll still walk her to her door, though, where they wouldn't be seen. They cross the street and are halfway up the driveway, a few metres from Kennedy's door, when Mom's head appears over the fence.

"Hi Kennedy. Hi Jordan." Dressed all in black, her new "theatre uniform," Mom's holding a clump of upended weeds in her gloved hand. "How was the beach?"

"Great, Mrs. Baines," pipes up Jordan. After such a long, silent walk, Kennedy is startled to hear his voice again.

"See you soon," he says, waving to Kennedy as he trots sideways down the drive.

"Bye," she sighs, watching him go. He's hurrying now, as if he knows his retreat will be watched. She guesses he's blushing. God, he's even more self-conscious than she is.

"Kennedy, your dad can use a table setter," says Mom.

"I want to shower first."

"After dinner, please. It'll be ready in five minutes."

"What's wrong with Liam?"

"He emptied the dishwasher today, so you can set the table," Mom says irritably.

"Fine." Kennedy knows when not to push it. Then she remembers. "Did you find out when your friend Judith's coming?"

"July twenty-second. For a week."

"And is her son coming?" Kennedy tries to make it sound like she wishes he weren't.

"Him too. Sorry, you'll just have to share your space."

Colin, thinks Kennedy, as she hangs her wet towel and suit in the bathroom. A naked English Colin in my shower. Stop it, she tells herself, but the picture is already full blown.

After dinner, while waiting for Sarina and Miko to arrive, Kennedy takes her keyboard from the closet and sets it on her desk. What to play? Maybe the love theme from *Titanic*. She still loves that song after all these years, and it's in just the right key for her range. While performing her palate stretch followed by her breathing exercises, she makes sure her door is locked and her windows shut. Humming her scales, she sits before the keyboard. Her thoughts quiet even before her fingers touch the keys, and she can feel a vibration starting up in her body as if in anticipation of the sound it's about to make.

Her fingers ease into the opening bars. Not too fast, not too slow, *forte* on the first chord of each stanza. She sings a soft "*ah*" and begins to warm and open her throat. She drops down an octave and lets the note resonate in her chest. Then drops it down farther, into her belly. When the song starts, the sound rises effortlessly, fully formed.

"Every night in my dreams, I see you, I feel you. That is how I know you go on."

Back when she used to think Leonardo DiCaprio was hot, she would conjure his face as she sang this. Lately it's been Colin Firth as Mr. Darcy, but tonight it's a strange combination of faces, Jordan's tanned face plus a boy she's never seen. An eighteen-year-old English boy.

"Far across the distance and spaces between us, you have come to show you go on."

Singing has always felt like pre-language to her, the words only incidental to the heart of the song. When she sings, it's as if all her questions and confusions are being articulated and answered at the same time. And suddenly it's as if there's really nothing to have to figure out. She only has to be fully in this moment, filling the air with song. She closes her eyes, and as if by itself the sound grows bigger, taking her along with it.

"Near ... far ... wherever you are, I believe that the heart does go on."

She senses a vague tickle on her leg but it's too distant to bother her.

"Once ... more, you o-pen the door, and you're here in my heart, and my heart will —"

The tickle is moving up her leg and Kennedy suddenly registers what it is.

"Ah!" she bats at her leg and leaps from her chair. Her skin crawls as she watches an enormous wolf spider skitter along the floor. She grabs the cup reserved for spiders, holds her breath and quickly lowers it over the spider's ugly back. One black leg sticks out from under the rim, half crushed and moving agonizingly slow.

"Oh gross, I'm sorry," she says, lifting the edge for the tiny leg to drag itself under. She looks away. "Dad!" she yells, hoping he'll hear. "Dad!"

When she hears footsteps on the stairs, she unlocks and opens her door. "Could you please put this spider outside?" she says as he comes around the corner. His face is worried and he's out of breath.

"Is that all it is?" he says, obviously relieved.

Dad's never liked the idea of Kennedy living alone downstairs. Last fall he argued that Liam should be the one to get this room. "Girls should sleep close to their parents," he said to Mom, who mocked him, saying he was being "ridiculous and old-fashioned. Boys are just as vulnerable as girls and girls just as capable as boys," was her comeback.

Liam said he didn't want to change rooms. So Kennedy had stopped the arguing by saying she would prefer the downstairs room. Dad used to check the carport door each night, making sure it was locked. Sometimes he'd come down more than once. After a month or so, he started asking Kennedy to do it on her way to bed.

"Thanks, Dad," she says as the spider cup is airlifted outside.

"No problem." He looks at the keyboard. "Was that you singing? I thought it was the radio."

"It was me." Kennedy smiles. Did she really sound that good?

9

Sarina and Miko arrive for the hike together. Miko is dressed head to toe in white: white sneakers, white jeans, white shirt and white hoodie. Probably her parents' suggestion, so she'll stand out in the dark. She looks adorable and reminds Kennedy of Tory's Hello Kitty doll. Sarina's wearing shorts, a tank top, no jacket and platform sneakers.

"You're going to be cold, Sarina," says Kennedy. "Want a jacket or something?"

"Yeah, sure, I guess." Sarina sounds distracted.

"Oh, I meant to bring my water bottle," says Miko.

"We've got one," says Kennedy.

Upstairs, Dad is at the kitchen table playing Old Maid with Tory. Mom has left for her rehearsal, saying she'd be home by eleven, which seems awfully late to Kennedy.

"You girls should take a flashlight," Dad suggests. "The forest canopy blocks the light. Gets dark sooner than you think."

"We'll come down by the road," says Kennedy. "There'll be enough cars going up and down."

"And it'll get cold too," he adds, "when the sun goes down."

"We're taking jackets."

"Hey," calls Liam, eavesdropping from the living room. "Watch out for cougars. They like to hunt at sundown, you know. Fifteen-year-old girls are like birthday cake to them. Devil's food cake with triple fudge icing. Hella smarties all over the —"

"We're scared now," says Kennedy.

"I'm a cougar," says Tory, putting down her cards to stand on the chair, lift her shirt and show off her striped belly. She's used a red marker this time. "A striped cougar." She looks at Kennedy as if daring her to correct her.

"Ooh, now *you're* scary," says Miko.

"You're not going to eat us, are you?" says Sarina, covering her face.

"No," says Tory. "I just ate a hamburglar."

Jackets tied around their waists, they head down Kennedy's street to a dirt path leading into Mount Doug Park. Having a giant wooded park, a rain forest, practically in their backyard is the best part about where they live, thinks Kennedy. Not to mention the incredible view from the top of the mountain. The paths in the park are cushioned with pine needles and the thick trunks of the Douglas fir covered with moss and ivy. There's green and more green everywhere you look. The ancient trees seem sentient to Kennedy, conscious, more like large patient animals than plants.

As Kennedy and her friends keep to the main path, they pass her favourite trail off to the left that runs parallel to the farm fields of Blenkinsop Valley. In the spring, that path is lined with trilliums and Easter lilies. The romantic landscape reminds her of Elizabeth's walks in *Pride and Prejudice*. Maybe when Colin comes she'll show him around the neighbourhood, take him down that path. She could suggest an evening hike like this, maybe even take a picnic ...

"Remember in grade seven when we had to stay in at recess because of the cougar sighting?" says Miko, pulling Kennedy from her daydream.

"Yeah," says Sarina. "I remember it was sunny out after days of rain, and I was pissed off."

"What about that story of the eight-year-old girl a cougar carried off by the neck. Like a cat carrying its kitten," says Miko. "Can you even imagine?"

"I remember the kid was okay except for some cuts around her neck," joins in Kennedy.

"Yeah, lucky."

"And then there was that like sixty-year-old man who was getting mauled and managed to kill the cat with his pocket knife," Miko continues.

"Yeah, he slit its throat," adds Kennedy. "I read that half the attacks in Canada are on Vancouver Island."

"Stop it," says Sarina, edging closer to Kennedy. "You guys are freaking me out."

"My dad says it's super rare to ever see one," says Kennedy. "So rare that the Natives called them ghost cats."

"God, what would you do if one jumped from that tree?" says Miko, pointing.

"Run like hell," answers Sarina, glancing over her shoulder.

"No, you should never run," says Kennedy. "That only triggers their attack response because you're fleeing just like food. And you're never supposed to turn your back."

"We were told at Camp Thunderbird to yell at them," offers Miko, "or sing really loud. To prove you're smarter than them." She nudges in between Kennedy and Sarina and links her arms with theirs. "Lions and tigers and bears, oh my," she starts, singing off-key.

"Lions and tigers and bears," they all sing together, stepping in time to the song. "Lions and tigers and bears."

Dust kicks up under their feet and then Sarina stops the line. "No, we should replace lions with cougars. Bears make sense, but what else is dangerous on Vancouver Island?"

"Rats," says Miko, scrunching up her little nose.

"How about weasels?" suggests Kennedy. "Weasels and cougars and bears."

"Weasels are cute," says Miko.

"No, they're not," says Sarina.

"My cousin has a ferret named Jake. He's cute."

"Think of wolverines," says Kennedy. "They may be cute but they're deadly."

"'Wolverine' is too long a word. Let's use weasels," says Sarina.

They restart the song and step.

"Weasels and cougars and bears, oh my!" The one-line song goes nowhere fast and they fall out of line, laughing.

"I love the other song Judy Garland sings in *The Wizard of Oz*," says Miko.

Kennedy knows from Miko's family's video collection that they're huge fans of Judy Garland. "'Somewhere Over the Rainbow'?" asks Kennedy. She has the sheet music to it, used to play it a lot and sing along.

"Yeah," agrees Sarina. "You sing it, Kennedy."

"Yeah, I've never heard you sing," urges Miko.

"No way," says Kennedy. "I'm too shy to sing in front of people."

For some reason Sarina seems ticked off by this. "We're not people. We're your friends."

"Maybe someday."

"What if your life depended on it?" Sarina says, a challenge in her voice.

"But it doesn't, does it?" Kennedy comes back, surprised at how snarky Sarina is these days.

"It doesn't matter," says Miko. "How much farther to the top?" she asks, changing the subject.

As the path steepens, it requires more breath and effort and the conversation dwindles. Rising out of the tall Douglas firs, the upper part of Mount Doug is covered in stunted Garry oaks. Kennedy studies their arthritic-looking branches. Ideal perches for cougars, she thinks, their goldy-green leaves the perfect camouflage. She imagines one stretched out along a branch observing them like a bored house cat. Only bigger. She wonders if a cougar's head is clam-shaped, like Mojo's.

The path has disappeared now, and they climb craggy rocks that flicker bronze in the sun. Manoeuvring hand- and footholds, they climb and climb and finally reach the top, sweating freely. They veer away from the parking area and tourists, find a grassy knoll farther west and pass the water bottle around. The sun sits low in a sky striped with pink clouds.

"God, it's beautiful," says Miko.

Kennedy and Sarina nod in silent agreement. Below them, the view stretches out in all directions: Cordova Bay to their left, the Sooke hills to their right, the suburbs rolling out in front all the way to the Victoria skyline, then there's the strait running across to the Olympic Mountains in Washington State.

"Life looks like no big deal from up here," says Sarina, quietly.

"Yeah," agrees Kennedy.

"I wish I could fly," Miko says. Then closing her eyes, Miko lifts her arms in the air as if to ride the gentle currents of wind.

"Me too." Sarina starts to do the same.

"Like in dreams," says Kennedy, closing her eyes and lifting her arms. As strands of hair whip softly against her face, she takes a deep breath and feels her expanding diaphragm push against her ribs. She suddenly feels like belting out Dorothy's song over the valley below, vibrating the air with her voice. She imagines the song dispersing the clouds and continuing into space ad infinitum, like ripples on water. But she knows she wouldn't dare and swallows the feeling instead. Her arms feel heavy now, as if weighed down with inhibitions, and she lowers them.

PAIN #14: SELF-CONSCIOUSNESS

It sucks, thinks Kennedy, feels so cowardly, so limiting. She imagines that, instead of the freeing sound of her voice going out into the universe, her thoughts of self-consciousness are now out there, adding to some big miserable collective self-consciousness that keeps people from expressing how they really feel, from being spontaneous and brave.

She opens her eyes to see Sarina and Miko riding the wind like stationary birds. Sarina's eyes are scrunched so tight it looks as though she's holding back from crying. Kennedy leans over close to her ear.

"Are you okay?" she asks softly, so Miko won't hear.

Sarina's eyes snap open.

"I'm fine. What's wrong with *you*?"

Kennedy's hurt must have registered on her face because Sarina takes it back.

"Sorry, Kennedy. I didn't mean it. You just startled me, is all."

Kennedy can tell she's lying and feels even more hurt, but this time doesn't show it. "That's okay," she says, which is not what she really wants to say, and she feels cowardly again.

"I think something's in my eye," says Sarina. "Dirt or something."

More cover-up, thinks Kennedy. What is it that Sarina won't talk about?

"Blink and rub the eye toward your nose," says Miko, oblivious.

"I've got a riddle," Sarina says, rubbing her eye while changing the topic. "Let's sit down, my legs are tired."

"Oh, I love riddles," says Miko eagerly. They move a few stones and sticks aside to make a place for themselves on the dry grass.

"You have to ask yes or no questions to try and figure it out. Okay?"

Miko nods, ready.

"Every day a man goes to visit his friend who lives in an apartment building on the thirteenth floor," Sarina begins.

"Buildings don't have thirteenth floors," Miko jumps in.

"Fourteenth, then," says Sarina. "And every time he gets in the elevator, he pushes button number nine, gets out on the ninth floor and walks five flights to his friend's apartment. When he leaves his friend's place, he just takes the elevator all the way down."

"The elevator's broken?" says Miko. "The friend lives in a penthouse?"

"No and no."

Into the momentary silence, a raven makes a mad cackling sound, loud and uninhibited.

"Is he blind?" asks Miko.

"No."

"Is there somebody else in the elevator with him?" asks Kennedy as the raven emerges from behind them to soar out over the valley.

"No."

"Is he superstitious?" asks Miko.

"No."

"Can he reach the higher buttons?" says Kennedy, and Sarina slowly shakes her head but smiles encouragingly.

"Did someone cut his legs off?" blurts Miko.

"No, he has legs. But you're close."

They sit quietly for a minute, Miko stealing worried looks at Kennedy.

"He's a midget?" says Kennedy, and Miko frowns at her.

"Yes," says Sarina, lying back on the dry grass.

"And he can't reach past the ninth-floor button," finishes Miko.

"One of the kids my dad coaches told him that one." Sarina looks sad suddenly.

What's bothering her? Kennedy wonders. She looks out at the view and sees that the sun's about to set.

"Look — the sun," she announces, and they all watch in silence as the fiery ball seems to swell in a slow-motion dance, turning the horizon a brilliant orange. A minute later, the sun sinks out of sight.

"Wow," whispers Sarina.

Their eyes remain glued to the darkening sky as if by some freak chance the sun might reappear. Then Sarina, never short on ideas, suggests they lie in a triangle with their heads on each other's stomachs. "I did this in some drama camp. If someone laughs it's totally contagious."

As soon as they have themselves arranged, Miko is laughing and jiggling Kennedy's head in the hollow of her stomach.

"What's so funny?" asks Kennedy.

"Nothing." They all laugh at this, which makes them laugh even harder. When their laughing starts to slack off, their lungs have to work to catch their breath, which causes their stomachs to spout little puffs of air and abruptly jar each other's heads. They can't help but start up again. It's a good twenty minutes before the novelty wears off and stomachs and lungs begin to settle. They lie quietly, staring at the sky.

"Stars are coming out," says Miko. "Make a wish and whoever's the first one to see a shooting star, her wish will come true." She states this as if it's fact.

Kennedy always wishes the same thing in these situations: for every being on the planet to be truly content. She figures that just about covers it. Especially Mom, she adds to her wish tonight. May she be content with what she already has.

"Hey, there's this kid coming to stay with us," Kennedy says into the sky.

"Who?" asks Miko.

"An old college roommate of my mom's named Judith is coming with her son, all the way from England. They're going to spend the last week of July with us. He's seventeen or eighteen."

"That's no kid," says Sarina.

"What's his name?" asks Miko.

"Colin."

"As in Colin Firth?" teases Sarina.

"I don't know his last name," Kennedy says, smiling.

"Ooh, a grade twelve. Or maybe he's graduated already. Is he cute?" asks Miko.

"I wouldn't know, I've never met him. But he'll be sleeping in the rec room and sharing my bathroom."

"What will Jordan say?" says Miko.

"He's going to be on vacation then, isn't he?" asks Sarina, her eyebrows dancing. "Just make sure, Miss Kennedy, that Colin doesn't sleepwalk into your room at night."

Their laughter rushes around the triangle of bodies, a single unbroken laugh.

10

"I got a lubby bunch a poconuts ... dee da ba duh," sings Tory. She wiggles her fingers in the air to accompany the dee da ba duh, as if playing an invisible piano. "Here they are jus sanding in a row ... bom, bom, bom ... big one, sall one, some as big as your head." She emphasizes the word "head" with stiff hands on either side of her own and abruptly stops the song, smiling an expectant smile, waiting for a reaction.

Everyone laughs politely. Colin's mother Judith laughs the loudest. Colin smiles coolly on one side of his face only. Mother and son have just arrived a half hour ago and are sitting in Kennedy's living room having a beer and Coke respectively. Liam is at the computer playing with the sound off. When Dad offered drinks, Colin asked for a beer. "Sorry, drinking age is nineteen in these parts," Dad said, and Kennedy had almost died with embarrassment. Tory's the only one who doesn't feel the awkwardness of entertaining strangers, conveniently filling any gaps in the conversation with her attention-getting repertoire.

"I have a princess dress," Tory says to Judith. "And a

ballerina dress. Would you like me to put them on?"

"Oh yes, very much," says Judith, and Tory runs off.

"Then I'll dance for you," comes Tory's disappearing voice.

"She's adorable," Judith says. She glances from Dad to Mom, then back to Dad where her glaze lingers as if she's having trouble focusing. "She looks so much like you, Leslie," she says, her eyes still on Dad.

Kennedy looks at her mom for a reaction, for an admission of guilt, but Mom's smiling, looking perfectly at ease. She tries to force her brain to remember what colour hair that Fredericton director had, but her attention returns to Colin, who, sitting across from her on the couch, runs his fingers through his dark blond hair.

Speaking of adorable, he truly is, and she's trying not to stare. He hasn't said much, looks bored — jet-lagged, no doubt — but he is even more gorgeous than the boy of her imaginings. Brushed back from his squarish, zit-free face, soft curls ride the collar of his dark red shirt. Silk? His eyes are an intense blue, the colour of deep water, and his lips ... Colin is flush with lip. Shapely, full, beautiful lips. He seems older than seventeen, has got to be eighteen anyway. Definitely shaves. He looks so worldly, but then she remembers he's lived everywhere, so duh. His slender nose has a slight bump down its bridge and reminds her of Tory's treehouse slide. And it is quite possibly as long as her own. She discreetly touches her own nose as if to apologize for slandering it so often. Because no one, Kennedy states to herself, would not think this guy's hot.

Mojo rubs against her chair and Kennedy reaches down and picks her up. Mojo will give her something to do with her hands. She settles the cat in her lap with a few long strokes.

"Beautiful cat," says Judith, the fingers of her left hand thrumming her lap in a nervous way. She doesn't seem to realize she's doing it. "We have a cat, an unfriendly Siamese, who will gore you if you even think about petting him." Judith is a thin woman with darting black eyes. Her hair, dyed a coppery red, is cut in a sharp line with her chin. One side of it tends to swing forward over her left eye, as if she's hiding behind a little curtain. Kennedy knows Judith's the same age as her mom, forty-two, but the grooved lines crossing her brow and arching down from her lipsticked mouth make her look closer to Dad's age. Her nose is slightly redder than the rest of her face, and Kennedy wonders if she has a cold.

Mom starts telling Judith about the play she's involved in. Kennedy isn't the least bit interested and blocks her out. She glances back at Colin and, to her surprise, his eyes are there to meet hers. Incisive eyes that look the direct opposite of shy. He smiles at her, a sexy half-smile, and her entire body hums as if about to burst into song. She looks down at the cat on her lap and strokes harder. Mojo purrs loudly. Is Colin still looking at her?

Tory comes prancing back into the living room and proceeds to twirl in front of Judith, the white satin skirt of her princess dress billowing with air. For once, Kennedy is grateful for her sister's interruption.

"So, Colin," says her dad, leaning forward in his chair. "Nice to be finished high school?"

"A terrific relief." Colin's eyes flicker to his mother, who lowers hers to her beer.

"Any plans for what's next? Travel, university ..."

"Well, I guess the travelling's already begun," Colin answers, then looks away, over his shoulder at Liam on the computer.

It's a dismissive answer, cocky really, and Kennedy watches Dad's eyebrows rise before he settles back in his chair. Or maybe it just sounded cocky because of his accent. Brits sound superior despite themselves, thinks Kennedy. All those "ah" sounds. Colin's mom smiles apologetically at Dad and he returns her look with one of friendly commiseration. Suddenly her smile shifts to something more coy. What's she doing? Dad seems slightly confused and reaches for his drink. Judith turns quickly to Mom and asks if she's heard from any of their "chums" from college.

"Hey, Colin," says Liam. "Ever hear of the game Morrowind?"

"No, I haven't," Colin says in his chiselled English.

Kennedy pets Mojo so hard the cat meows, then leaps to the floor.

"Want to watch?" asks Liam.

"Sure thing," says Colin, flatly but beautifully.

Kennedy has the pleasure of watching Colin's tall, at least six-one, perfectly proportioned body stand and walk over to the computer with what she'd call graceful confidence. Mom taps Judith on the knee and with a little nod of her head indicates the boys' friendly interaction. Judith nods several exaggerated, weirdly overenthused nods. Kennedy feels sorry for Colin for having such a weird mother.

Kennedy remains glued to her chair, too shy to join the boys and not willing to leave the room as long as Colin's in it.

She listens to the music of Colin's voice as he asks Liam questions about the game. Tory is now drawing a picture, probably to show to Judith. Mom and Judith are reminiscing about the "good ol' days" when Dad asks if Stephan, Colin's father, will be meeting up with them at some point.

"Stephan can't get away right now, I'm afraid," says Judith. "Hate travelling without him, but then I do have Colin with me." She looks at her son with what Kennedy thinks is a phony smile, and Colin immediately announces that's he's "terribly lagged and wouldn't mind a lie-down."

A lie-down. Too great.

"Kennedy, sweetheart," says Mom. "Show Colin downstairs. I put extra towels in the bathroom cupboard and the bed is made, just needs to be pulled out. There's a couple of pillows on top of the bookshelf."

"Sure, Mom," she says, understanding that she must now move from the safety of her chair and talk to this godlike male specimen. Her adrenalin has kicked in and as she stands, her feet seem too far away to be trusted. She walks ahead of Colin toward the stairs, worrying with each step that her foot won't hit solid ground. Her tongue suddenly feels way too big for her mouth and she says nothing as she starts down the stairs as calmly as she can. Wearing low-cut jeans and a tank top that just happens to show off her waist, she imagines his eyes checking her out from behind. She can't tell if she's walking weirdly slow or at a normal pace. On the last carpeted step, her heel slips, causing her leg to jar, straight-kneed, onto the flagstone floor of the hall.

"Shit," says Kennedy under her breath.

"You all right?" comes Colin's lilting voice.

She dares look back at him, standing behind her on the stairs in his baggy navy shorts — linen? — and silken shirt with two buttons open at the collar. His face is in shadow and she can't tell where his eyes are looking.

"I'm fine, thanks," she says. "The rec room's this way." There, her tongue does work.

He picks up his suitcase by the front door, then grabs his brown leather jacket from the hall closet where Kennedy's dad had hung it. The jacket has a strong, almost tangy smell she can't quite place. In the rec room, she starts taking cushions off the couch bed in order to pull it out.

"Oh, don't bother with that," says Colin with his half-smile. "I'll do it later. I really just wanted to have a fag. Can we open a window or do I have to smoke outside?" He asks this without looking at her.

"Uh, sure, we can open a window," she says, and then thinks better of it. Mom's allergic. "Actually, I think my dad would prefer you smoke outside," she says instead, and feels like a complete dork.

Colin digs in the pocket of his jacket. "Sure thing," he says.

That was the smell, thinks Kennedy. Cigarettes. She'd heard from her math teacher, who spent the summer in Europe, that unlike here, it's still the norm to smoke over there.

He smiles a charming smile directly at her. "Care to join me?"

"Oh, I don't —"

"Not for a smoke, but to show me the yard or something?"

"Okay," she says, her cheeks lighting up with an embarrassed excitement. She feels all jumpy inside, like a little kid, and wants to skip ahead of him, pointing out things and asking him a hundred questions, one right after another.

He follows her outside into the carport, where the ping-pong table is set up. Liam had played with his friend Sam this afternoon and as usual hadn't folded it back up.

"You play?" asks Colin, lighting up a cigarette.

"Not that well, but yeah."

"I haven't played since I was a kid," he says. "Since living here, actually."

"Want to?" she offers, hoping to sound offhand, in case he thinks it's a dumb idea.

"I would," he says cheerfully, and Kennedy can't help but smile.

She finds the paddles and ball and he readies himself on the other side, cigarette dangling dangerously from his luscious lips. So cool.

"Let's just fool around first," she says, tossing the ball across the net. She hears what she just said and misses his return.

PAIN #15: SAYING STUPID THINGS

If only you could rewind certain moments and try again.

"Sorry." She retrieves the ball.

They play for a while, him laughing and smoking without hands, and Kennedy starts to relax. This is what it must be like having a big brother, she tells herself. A really cute big brother with a totally sexy voice. They decide to play an actual game to twenty-one. The score remains close throughout. Kennedy is relieved and proud that she's as good as him. And she might have won if Colin hadn't spiked the ball on his last two returns.

"Sorry to get tough there, I'm horribly competitive,"

he smiles. "Couldn't bear to lose to a ... how old are you?"

Kennedy hesitates. "Almost sixteen," she says and wonders just how stupid that sounded. She might as well have said "fifteen and three-quarters," though that would have been a lie too. She's fifteen and thirty-four days.

"Couldn't bear to lose to a young lady," he says, "no matter how pretty she is."

He smiles a totally brilliant smile, then his blue eyes flash down to her exposed waist and back to her face. Kennedy is so flustered that she laughs stupidly, right out loud.

"You think I'm joking?" he says.

She can't begin to respond.

"Because I mean it," he says in a voice not unlike Mojo's purr.

No, thinks Kennedy, her heart racing, Colin is definitely not shy.

The door opens and Dad steps outside. "Thought I heard some ping-pong going on." Her dad looks so uncool next to Colin, Kennedy is almost embarrassed for him. "Who won?"

Colin points to Kennedy just as Kennedy points to Colin. She sputters with laughter.

"A tie, maybe," Dad answers himself, his eyes flickering to the cigarette butt Colin put out on the carport floor. "Just seeing if Colin has all he needs down here."

"Your house is very accommodating, thank you," says Colin politely, though he doesn't sound very sincere.

"Good, good," says Dad, smiling at Kennedy before retreating inside.

"I was supposed to make a call ... that I forgot about," Kennedy says quickly. She has to get out of here before she ruptures something. "Thanks for the game."

"Let's play again sometime."

"Sure. Liam's better at it than me," she adds. "Maybe he'll play with you."

Colin just stands there, nodding and smiling at her. She goes inside, heads for her room and locks the door behind her. She falls onto her bed and covers her mouth to stop herself from screaming. He was totally flirting with her. He's gorgeous. Oh my god, she has to call Sarina.

She makes Sarina promise to come by tomorrow.

"It's too much to be around him alone," says Kennedy.

Sarina has a dentist appointment at eleven but promises to come over right after. "Maybe Colin could borrow your dad's car and we could go downtown. See the buskers and go to Zombie's. I love their pizza."

"I doubt Dad would let him, but maybe," says Kennedy.

"Ask your mom."

The only way Kennedy can get from her bedroom to the bathroom or from her bedroom to the upstairs is through the rec room. When she makes her way to the bathroom to get ready for bed, Colin is already lying on the pulled-out sofa, flicking through TV channels. He's wearing his shorts. Nothing else. Kennedy says hi as nonchalantly as possible, while noting the little diamond of curls in the centre of his perfectly formed chest.

"Hi, Kennedy," he says back. "Different stuff on the

telly here. You'd think I'd have some memory from having lived here, but I don't."

"Mmm," Kennedy responds dumbly. "I'm just going to use the bathroom and go to bed."

She slips into the bathroom. "So hot," she mouths to her reflection in the mirror, then bites her lower lip to keep herself from groaning.

She sits on the toilet to pee and then, afraid he might be able to hear, reaches over to run the water tap as camouflage. She'll be totally constipated by the time he leaves, she jokes to herself. She takes out her contacts and puts them in their cleaning solution, then realizes she doesn't want Colin to see her in her glasses. Her eye-shrinking glasses. Her Mr. Magoo glasses, as Liam calls them.

PAIN #16: BEING BLIND

Kennedy has worn glasses for as long as she has memory. She was one of those goofy-looking near-sighted little kids with the bottle-bottom lenses and pink frames. It wasn't until grade six that the optometrist, and Dad, finally allowed her to get contacts. She figures she can make it from here to the bedroom without her glasses and carries them hidden in her hand.

Emerging from the bathroom, Kennedy smiles at the blurry figure on the couch. "Goodnight."

"Goodnight, Kennedy," says Colin, his refined English all the more resonant as Kennedy's ears make up for her loss of sight. "Hey, who are you named for? The former president?"

"No, it's my mom's maiden name." She continues to walk toward her room, trying not to squint at the cloudlike floor.

"That's good. It would be strange to name someone

after a family with so much bad luck."

"No kidding," she says. "Goodnight again."

"Goodnight, lucky Kennedy."

She melts inside just a little, before her hand misjudges the doorknob and she has to awkwardly catch herself. At least I didn't walk right into it, she tells herself. Back in the safety of her bedroom, she puts on her nicest pyjamas, the blue satin shorts and tank top from La Senza that Mom bought her for her birthday.

She picks up *Pride and Prejudice* and gets into bed. She's coming up to her absolute favourite part, when an agitated Mr. Darcy cannot contain his repressed passion for Elizabeth any longer and abruptly proposes to her. But Kennedy can't focus on the words. Her entire being is tuned to the person on the other side of her wall. She has Mr. Darcy's proposal memorized, in any case: *"In vain have I struggled. It will not do. My feelings will not be repressed. You must allow me to tell you how ardently I admire and love you."*

Kennedy listens for any sounds Colin might make, her mind going back over everything that he said tonight. She needs to ask Sarina what she thinks of him. But Jordan. This really isn't fair to him. She pictures Jordan on the beach in Parksville, sitting beside a pretty girl in a bikini, a girl who's shorter than him, a year younger, and who likes everything about him. Kennedy hears the TV shut off and holds her breath, listens for possible clearing of his throat, a sigh, snoring sounds. She almost laughs aloud, remembering what Sarina said about him sleepwalking into her room at night. A minute later, she hears footsteps. What? A light knock on her door?

"Kennedy," someone whispers.

She doesn't know whether to pretend she's asleep or to get up and answer it. The knock comes again, slightly louder this time, and she's up, taking off her glasses and putting on her robe. Her skin feels electrified as she opens the door and squints into the dark.

"Sorry, sweetheart," comes her dad's whispery voice. "I saw your light on and just wanted to say goodnight."

"Oh, that's okay," she says, her tensed shoulders dropping an inch. "Goodnight, Dad."

"Okay, sleep well. See you in the morning." He reaches over and strokes the side of her cheek down to her chin.

She shuts her door and gets back into bed. Why did he do that? Dad never comes down and says goodnight anymore. Of course, there's not usually a half-naked guy who shaves, sleeping in the rec room. She smiles and curls up on her side. It's okay, Dad, she's a big girl now. She can handle it.

It takes Kennedy twenty minutes to decide what to wear before she dares to come out of her bedroom. When she emerges, she's relieved to see Colin's messed bed and him not in it. The air smells strongly of cigarette smoke and she notices the window's open. The sound of a pee stream hits her ears and she's both intrigued and a little grossed out as her strong visual imagination kicks in. Willow once said that you can tell the size of a guy's thing by his hands: that the measure from his wrist to the end of his ring finger corresponded to its length and the thickness of his palm correlated to its width. Kennedy didn't ask how Willow learned this. She'd heard the nose theory before but not the hand theory. Then just last week on the radio, some researcher was interviewing women about whether size really matters. The conclusion was that length didn't matter but width did. They didn't say anything about the love factor.

Kennedy suddenly feels uneasy and self-conscious and wants to run upstairs to use another bathroom. But her contacts are in this one so she waits, pretending not to listen to the flush, the brushing of teeth and finally the buzz of an electric shaver roaming over and under those lips. The door opens and there he is, in black jeans and a sexy undershirt. His smoothly muscled body couldn't be more perfect. She inhales sharply.

"Oh, sorry to keep you waiting," he says.

"Sleep well?" she blurts.

"Brilliant, you?"

"Fine, thanks."

Their arms brush as she moves past. Goose bumps sprout from her head to her toes.

Over one of Dad's big weekend breakfasts, Liam asks Colin some of the questions Kennedy would have asked if she weren't so self-conscious.

"Are the schools really that much harder in England? 'Cause you went to school here too, didn't you?"

"Grades five through seven."

"Yes," confirms Colin's mother. "We lived down in Cadboro Bay. He went to Frank Hobbs."

Kennedy thinks Judith is acting more normal this morning, until she asks Kennedy, who has sat down next to Dad, to change seats with her.

"And to answer your question," Colin continues, "schooling in England is much, much harder."

"Poor Colin nearly wept when he came home that first day with his homework list," Judith says.

"I complained," corrects Colin.

"So what do you like to do?" Liam asks.

"Oh, the regular," says Colin.

"Do you play soccer? I mean football? Soccer football? Foot ..."

Watching Liam hold back from taking that one for a ride, Kennedy stifles a laugh.

"Used to. Got tired of it."

"Colin was a star player at his secondary school. His coach said he could have played pro," Judith boasts to Dad as if it were her accomplishment. She gives his hand a fluttery pat.

"I play keeper on a team here," says Liam, suddenly sounding as jaded as Colin. "It's all right."

"Do you drive?" Colin asks Kennedy.

"Kennedy's only just turned fifteen," says Liam. "You can't even get your learner's here until sixteen."

Thanks Liam, thinks Kennedy.

"Colin, you could borrow our car —" Mom starts to say. She looks to be wearing even more makeup than usual. Why?

"Well, I don't know," says Dad, putting down his fork.

"Actually, he can't," interrupts Judith. "Silly Colin forgot to bring his licence, didn't you, darling? Left it in his pants at home," she says with an ugly forced laugh. Colin says nothing. "But maybe, Colin, you could call one of your old friends, say Elliot, and see if he can take you kids around. His mother assured me Elliot would love to see you again."

Colin looks impatient. "Certainly."

"I have his number in my purse."

"My friend Sarina's coming over this afternoon," says Kennedy. "Maybe we could go downtown and see some buskers, get some pizza ..."

"Sounds fine." He gives her a *let's get out of here* look and Kennedy is utterly flattered. "I'll call Elliot after breakfast," he says. "My old mate."

Dad offers to drive them downtown himself and Kennedy's quick to say, "Thanks, Dad, but if Colin's friend can't drive, we can always take the bus."

"Can I come?" asks Liam.

"Me too!" says Tory, mournfully, through a mouthful of waffle.

Colin's eyes fix on his plate of eggs and sausage.

He can't take much more of this, thinks Kennedy. She has to say something, but what?

"Liam, I'll take you and a friend downtown tomorrow afternoon. You too, Tory," offers Dad. Kennedy gives him a grateful smile and he smiles weakly back.

After helping with the dishes, Kennedy looks for Colin downstairs. By the open door to the carport, she hears the fast click of a ping-pong game. The table's folded up on one side and he's playing solo.

Colin stops playing when he sees her pass. "Is there a phone downstairs?"

"There's one in my room," she says, and it just so happens she's heading that way.

"Mind if I use it to ring this fellow Elliot?" he asks, following her into her bedroom.

"No, go ahead." Feigning purpose, she picks up her book.

"What you reading?" he asks.

"Jane Austen."

"A dead Brit, eh?"

"Yeah, she's great."

"Wouldn't know, but sorry not to have been related."

Kennedy's not exactly sure what he means by this. Reaping the money from her success?

"God, I haven't seen old Elliot since I was thirteen." His long fingers hold up the piece of paper with Elliot's number. "He was an odd sort then. Can't imagine what he's like now," he says, punching in the number. "But if he has a car ... Hello!" His grudging tone changes to pure charm. "Is this Elliot? It's me, Colin Bernard, in town from England."

Colin turns his back to Kennedy, and although he's in *her* room she feels as if she should leave. She quietly takes her book outside to the trampoline. It's one of her favourite and most comfortable reading spots. She's often thought it would be the perfect place to make out at night, under the cover of dark. In fact, she's fairly sure Willow and Graham were out here during the party. Graham probably spray-painted the canoe on his way back inside.

She opens her book. Elizabeth has just rejected Mr. Darcy's proposal and he is stunned and insulted: *"And this is all the reply which I am to have the honour of expecting! I might, perhaps, wish to be informed why, with so little endeavour at civility, I am thus rejected ..."*

"I might as well enquire," replied she, *"why with so evident a design of offending and insulting me, you chose to tell me that you liked me against your will, against your reason, and even against your character? Was not this some excuse for incivility, if I was uncivil?"*

Kennedy is always thrilled by how nobly and eloquently Elizabeth stands up for herself in the presence of Mr. Darcy, whose "station in life" is so much higher than hers. *"But ... do you think that any consideration would tempt me to accept the man, who has been the means of ruining, perhaps for ever, the happiness of a most beloved sister?"* Then Elizabeth throws at him his unpardonable dealings with the handsome Mr. Wickham, which has *"reduced him to his present state of poverty."*

"My faults, according to this calculation, are heavy indeed! But perhaps ... these offences might have been overlooked, had not your pride been hurt by my honest confession of the scruples that had long prevented my forming any serious design ... Could you expect me to rejoice in the inferiority of your connections?" But the clincher, thinks Kennedy, rolling onto her stomach, is Elizabeth's swift, backboned response: *"You are mistaken, Mr. Darcy, if you suppose that the mode of your declaration affected me in any other way, than as it spared me the concern which I might have felt in refusing you, had you behaved in a more gentleman-like manner."*

Touché. And oh, the sparks between them. Kennedy drops her head into the book. *Pride and Passion*, it could have been called.

"Kennedy. There you are."

She looks up, but after reading with the sun in her eyes, Colin's nothing but a black blob coming toward her. "Hi. Just reading," she says.

"Got a car. You and your friend want to hit big downtown Victoria?"

"Sounds great." Kennedy hasn't missed the cynicism in his voice. "Victoria must be tiny compared to London."

"And a whole lot cleaner," he says, as if to make up for

the former. With one leap he's up on the trampoline and bouncing her onto her back.

"Ahh!" she can't help cry, and his hand is there pulling her up.

"Come on. Can I break this thing?" he says, jumping again.

"Not likely." His jumping bucks the trampoline and forces her to jump too.

She bounces around the outside edge, giving him the middle. But then he bounces too close to her feet, forcing her into the air and off balance. She lands awkwardly, falling against his chest. He steadies her in his arms, while her hands just happen to have gripped onto his muscled forearms. She can smell his musky deodorant.

"Sorry," she says.

"My fault," he says, his hands slipping away. Hers, reluctantly, do the same.

"Elliot's coming by around two."

"Good, fine," says Kennedy, trying to regain some composure. "Sarina will be here by then." She climbs down the ladder of the trampoline and he leaps over the side to land beside her.

"Sarina," he repeats. "Sounds like a witch."

Kennedy laughs and glances shyly up at him. His eyes are right there. Seductive and dangerous and totally thrilling.

As soon as they're inside, Kennedy runs upstairs to her parents' room to call Sarina on her cell. Nobody answers. She's probably in the dentist chair with her mouth open. It's okay, Kennedy reassures herself, she'll be here before two.

At quarter to two Sarina's dad's car pulls into the drive. Kennedy watches from her bedroom window as Sarina gets out and slams the car door, her face rigid with anger.

"Sarina," her dad calls out his window, but Sarina ignores him and walks toward the rec room door.

When Kennedy answers the door, Sarina's dad is still sitting there behind the wheel, eyes closed, leaning back on the headrest.

"Does your dad need to talk to you?" Kennedy asks, and Sarina pushes past without answering.

Kennedy looks from Sarina to her dad and back to Sarina. She slowly closes the door.

"What's going on?"

Sarina jerks her head to the side as if too overwhelmed to speak.

"Come in my room." Kennedy leads the way and locks the door behind them. She hears Sarina's car finally pulling out of the drive. "Sarina," she says firmly, "you have to tell me what's going on with you."

They sit together on the edge of the bed. When Sarina's eyelids flutter, staving off tears, Kennedy takes her hand. Her friend's head falls to her chest and the tears come. Soon she's crying so hard her shoulders are shaking and she's hiccuping back sobs. Kennedy squeezes Sarina's hand harder but doesn't say anything. She'll wait until her friend's ready to talk. After several minutes, Sarina is catching her breath and reaching for the box of tissues on Kennedy's dresser. She blows her nose and looks up at Kennedy, her eyes and nose red.

"I'm sorry," she says, smiling a thin smile.

"Don't apologize," says Kennedy. "But you'll feel better if you tell someone."

"I hate him," Sarina sniffs. "I hate them."

"Who?" Kennedy says gently.

"My mom and dad."

Sarina's mother was dynamic, creative and outgoing, a lot like Sarina. She was short too, like Sarina. The way they joked and laughed together, Kennedy always thought they seemed more like sisters than mother and daughter. Her dad was a jokey, easy-going kind of guy. Always had a joke to tell. They seemed like a tight-knit threesome and Kennedy often envied Sarina her only-child status.

Sarina takes an audible breath. "They're separating." Her head drops again but she doesn't cry.

Kennedy's shocked and doesn't know how to respond.

Sarina lifts her head and looks at Kennedy through teary eyes.

"My dad wants a divorce."

Kennedy recalls a drunk Sarina sitting up in this very bed calling out "two houses." Is this what she meant? Kennedy knows so many kids whose parents aren't together anymore. Chase and Willow. Sarah across the street. What's the stat? Fifty percent? She wonders if divorce existed in nineteenth-century England. She flashes on Mom kissing another man but quickly blinks the image away.

"That's so awful." She strokes Sarina's hand in hers, stroking her own in the process.

"Dad says he just doesn't love her anymore. How can ..." Sarina closes her eyes and takes a breath. "Does love just stop like that?"

"You know, maybe it's just a phase, a midlife thing, and it'll pass."

"I don't think so. Dad just told me that he found a place and is moving out at the end of the month. It's so confusing ..." She doesn't finish her sentence.

Kennedy's gut has twisted into a bulky knot. So this is what it feels like, she thinks.

"Sometimes I think he doesn't like that Mom makes more money than him. That he feels left behind in some way. She's always so busy and travels so much ... I don't know."

"Have you told him that?"

"No way."

"What does your mom say?"

"First she was in shock and now she's just furious. She thinks there must be someone else."

The knot in Kennedy's stomach tightens. She hears the doorbell ring and looks out her window. A taxi is sitting in the driveway. Is Judith going somewhere?

"What time is it?" ask Sarina, drying her eyes on her sleeve.

"It's two."

"Oh god, I have to fix my face. I must look rabid or something."

"Do you still want to go? We could hang out here if you'd rather. Take a walk?"

"No, I need distraction. This guy Colin sounds like a distraction. Can't wait to meet him," she says, forcing a smile, and Kennedy wants to cry too. Sadness doesn't suit Sarina. "I'll be disappointed if you've been pulling my leg." Sarina feigns her leg being pulled and falls off the bed onto the floor.

Kennedy laughs and gives her a hand up. The doorbell rings again.

"I should probably answer that."

"I'll be in the bathroom," says Sarina.

When Kennedy steps into the front hall, Colin is already opening the door.

"You threw in the towel, eh?" Colin is circling his hand around his head. "Look like a regular dirt hippie now."

He's blocking the doorway so Kennedy can only see half a blue-jeaned leg. She hears Elliot laugh, a cautious laugh. "And you haven't changed, I see."

Colin snickers and steps back, knocking into Kennedy.

"Oh, sorry girl, didn't see you," he says. "Kennedy Baines, meet Elliot Narwin, or Narwhal as we used to call him back in grade whatever." Colin grabs a handful of his own hair and pulls it up to the ceiling.

"Nice to meet you," says Elliot, reaching out his hand.

He looks younger than Colin, his rather serious face offset by eyes like a girl's — large with thick black lashes that curl up the way Kennedy wishes hers would.

"You too." She shakes his hand. Colin is standing so close to her now she can feel his body heat.

The narwhal thing must refer to those head buns the Sikh kids wear. She'd never seen that sort of headdress back in Fredericton, and for an entire month after the move, thought the Punjabi boy in her class was a girl. Elliot's skin is paler than the Sikhs she knows. His hair is tied back in a ponytail and she wonders how far it hangs down his back.

"Sarina's using the washroom. I'll tell my mom we're leaving," she says. "Be right back."

Halfway upstairs, she catches Colin's voice and the words "double date."

She can't tell what tone of voice he said it in, joking or serious?

"Young" is all she can catch of Elliot's quieter response, and she's instantly offended. Girls mature a lot faster than boys, she argues in her head.

"We're going," she announces to Mom and Judith, who are sitting on the deck drinking tall glasses of what looks like iced tea. Or is it beer?

"Have fun," says Mom. "You have money?"

"Yes."

"Elliot's here?" Judith puts her glass down with a clumsy thud and cranes her neck to look past Kennedy.

"Yeah, downstairs," Kennedy says, then turns to see him coming up behind her.

His walk is loose and easy, as if his joints are made of air. He walks right past her toward Judith. Now she can see that his hair, thick and shiny as oil paint, hangs almost to his waist.

"Hi, Mrs. Bernard," he says, like a regular adult.

"Elliot, is that you?" Judith is standing up to greet him and they shake hands. "Wow, you've grown, to say the least."

Elliot angles himself toward Mom as if to remind Judith of her manners.

"Oh yes. Leslie, this is Elliot."

He takes Mom's hand with a small bow of his head.

Suck-up, thinks Kennedy, anxious to get going. She wonders what Colin's doing.

"Oh, and tell your mom I'll give a call tomorrow. I'm still on English time, you see," Judith says. She sounds phony and affected to Kennedy. "But how are you? You graduated this year, I assume." Judith has her hand on Elliot's arm. Is she flirting with *him* too? Sick.

"Sure did."

"With honours, no doubt." Judith turns to Kennedy. "Elliot is a science and math whiz, skipped a grade somewhere along the line," she says, waving a sloppy hand.

Kennedy's amazed at how totally relaxed Elliot's body seems, his hands hanging languidly by his sides, as Judith tugs on him.

"And next year?"

"I've scholarships for U of T, McGill and here at UVic. Computer science."

"Good for you," says Mom.

Kennedy assesses his height. Assessing a guy's height has become an automatic reflex over the years. Just shy of six feet, she guesses.

"My parents wanted me to stay at home for my bachelor's so I'll be going to UVic this September."

He sounds like a nerd, she thinks, and looks nerdish too, in his white dress shirt with the rolled-up sleeves and those pale blue, slim-legged jeans. Slim legs went out of style how many years ago? Not that her secondhand cutoffs are exactly trendy. Kennedy hears talking in the carport below. Sarina and Colin?

"And your grandmother, she's well? Your father?"

Kennedy can't believe this conversation is continuing. It's as if Judith is obsessed. She's still hanging onto Elliot's arm.

"Grandmother's almost totally blind now but her ears make up for it. And Father's fine. He owns Royal Taxi now."

Judith looks surprised, or is it impressed?

"He had a rough year after 9-11, but business has more or less recovered by now."

Judith finally lets go of Elliot's arm and bats at the air as if ignoring the implications of what he just said.

"That's really ignorant and unfair," says Mom.

"Yes, it was." Elliot gives Mom a grateful smile.

Judith seems unable to think of what to say next and sits back down, reaching for her drink.

"Well, I guess we're off," says Elliot, tossing his head in Kennedy's general direction.

Fine, don't look at me, Mr. Scholarship, recalling the C she got in science this year.

PAIN #17: THROBHEADS

They make us average students look like idiots.

"Colin forgot his licence so he can't drive," Judith blurts.

"My dad doesn't allow any other drivers," Elliot says matter-of-factly.

"Yep, see ya," says Kennedy, hearing Sarina laughing now. "What time should we be back?"

"By dark would be good," says Judith, and Kennedy looks at her mother.

"Well, it gets dark late," Mom says, giving her some leeway.

"We won't be too late," Kennedy says.

"I'll make sure the girls are home by dark," says Elliot.

Kennedy rolls her eyes, wanting to elbow this parental suck in his smart ribs.

Looking like her cheery old self, Sarina is leaning on Elliot's cab and telling Colin about her mother spending time in London. Colin, sexy in wide-leg jeans and dark blue collared T-shirt to match his eyes, is smoking a cigarette. A backpack hangs from one shoulder.

"I guess we can go," says Kennedy.

"À la Royal Taxi," says Colin with a sweep of his hand.

On the car door, Kennedy discerns the faded lettering of Royal Taxi under the white outline of a crown. She's seen these taxis around town, and now that she thinks of it, they always seem to be driven by guys with turbans. Sikhs must stick together, she thinks, and wonders if this is out of choice or necessity. Colin makes a show of holding open the door for her and Sarina.

"So, driver, dare I sit in the back with these two beautiful young women?"

"What a flirt," Sarina mouths to Kennedy.

Kennedy glances at Elliot, whose eyes have gone as still as his hands. Maybe he doesn't appreciate being called "driver."

"Just kidding, old chum," says Colin. "That would be far too dangerous."

"For whom?" says Sarina.

Colin grins first at Sarina, then at Kennedy.

"For me, I hope," he says, then opens the passenger door, which creaks mournfully.

Inside the cab, Kennedy notices the old meter and walkie-talkie.

"Is this still a working cab?" asks Colin, taking the words out of her mouth.

"No. It's a family car now," says a totally humourless Elliot.

The car has a sweet, spicy smell, like cinnamon. She breathes it in and a wave of Colin's cigarette smoke hits her nose.

"No smoking in the car," says Elliot.

"Whatever you say." Colin takes a final drag and drops the butt out the window to smoulder on the carport floor. Dad won't be impressed.

Sarina pinches Kennedy's thigh and hooks her thumb at Colin. She shakes her hand in the sign meaning "hot." Kennedy widens her eyes and nods in agreement. Then Sarina points to Elliot with a wavering hand and whispers, "not bad either." Kennedy shrugs. He's too uptight to be cute, she thinks. Though he has nice eyes for sure.

"Shame it doesn't have those glass partitions with the little talking grille like they have in New York," says Colin.

"Seat belts on?" asks Elliot.

"No," Kennedy and Sarina answer in tandem, obediently seeking out buckles.

Feels like her father's driving them after all, thinks Kennedy.

"I promise," says Colin, "that if we see a bobby, I'll put mine on."

Sarina turns to Kennedy and mouths the word "bobby."

"Well, sorry, Colin, but we're not leaving this driveway until your belt's on," Elliot says. He sits back in his seat, one limp hand hanging over the steering wheel.

"Yes, sir, driver sir," says Colin as he buckles in. "You're still a serious bugger, Narwhal." Colin turns to address the girls. "My mother loved my playing with The Narl because he'd keep me out of trouble. Instead of making treacherous jumps for our bikes or heaving conkers at moving cars,

Elliot's idea of fun was to take apart the phone and put it back together."

Elliot is smiling now. He has a nice smile, thinks Kennedy. It changes his whole face.

"Remember the time we mixed up the receiver and talk piece and watched your grandmother answer the phone? She started yelling into it, then banging it on the table."

"She never trusted phones after that," laughs Elliot, pulling out of the drive.

Colin asks Elliot to update him on some of the other kids they used to hang with, and Kennedy, keeping her voice down, asks Sarina if she's feeling better.

Sarina nods. "It felt good to tell someone," she says and smiles a grateful smile. The pain is there in her eyes and Kennedy feels for her.

"Maybe your folks will work something out. Maybe your dad's pride is just hurt," Kennedy offers.

"I don't know," says Sarina, sounding sad again. Kennedy squeezes her hand and, sensing it's best to leave it be, changes the subject.

"This is cool," she whispers, and Sarina nods. Except for the odd ride home from school with Miko's brother, they never get to ride with older teenagers. It's either parents or the bus. As they cruise down Cedar Hill toward downtown, Kennedy finds the sense of freedom exhilarating. She studies the back of Colin's head, imagines touching his hair. Then she looks over at Elliot's proud profile. He resembles some sort of bird, she thinks, with his sleek hair and that gothic arch to his nose. A noble bird, she allows, an eagle maybe.

Colin flips on the radio and opera streams out of the speakers. Kennedy recognizes Charlotte Church. She thinks

Charlotte's okay, but she sings too much from her throat. Although some of her songs are awfully pretty.

"Hope that's your mother's station," says Colin, punching buttons to a rock station. Elliot doesn't respond. "Anybody care for a home brew?" asks Colin as he digs in his backpack.

They look identical to the beer that Kennedy's dad makes at the U-brew store and keeps under the stairs.

"Colin," says Kennedy, feeling bolder with Sarina by her side, "did you get those from our house?"

"Kennedy, please don't be mad at me," Colin says with a sheepish smile. "Your dad has about two hundred beer under those stairs. I didn't think he'd miss a measly four."

Elliot, staring ahead at the road, is shaking his head, his smile gone.

"I promise I won't do it again. It's just that I can't walk into a liquor store here like I can back home. I'm underage."

"You really promise?" says Kennedy, pretending to be firm.

"Cross my heart and hope to drink," he says, blinking his eyes boyishly.

Kennedy sighs and grabs a beer out of his hand. He smiles approvingly, holding her gaze. She stares right back, determined to hold out until he turns away first. He lowers his eyes and hands the other beer to Sarina. For the first time, Kennedy feels like Colin's equal and her nerves sting with the thrill of it.

"Dare I offer one to the driver?" Colin looks over at Elliot.

No way, thinks Kennedy.

"No, thanks," says Elliot, then surprises her by adding,

"I want to get downtown and park first. Save me one."

  · They ride with the music too loud to talk over: Eminem and his white rap. The beer is warm and bitter, but after the first few sips Kennedy doesn't mind the taste. She wonders what would happen if a cop stopped them. Underage kids drinking in a car has got to be bad. She's surprised Elliot's allowing it. At least there's no labels on these bottles. They could be drinking anything, really. She decides to keep her bottle low, just in case, and her eyes peeled for cops.

    Her favourite Hedley song comes on the radio and she wishes she had the guts to sing along, maybe impress Colin with her voice like Elizabeth does for Mr. Darcy in the BBC version. It's the best part of the movie because it's as if Elizabeth's voice has cast a spell on Darcy, and from that moment on, there's no turning back for him. She shyly hums a few notes, takes a swig of her beer — her dad's beer — and scans the road for police cars.

As they drive down Government Street toward the harbour, the cooler air carries the tangy smell of ocean. Elliot pulls into a convenient parking area along Wharf Street that's reserved for taxis only.

"Can you leave the car here?" asks Colin.

"Drivers do it all the time," says Elliot. "Can I have that beer now?"

"Bottoms up," says Colin, handing it over.

Kennedy is impressed by Elliot's casual cool. Watching him down his beer, she realizes she can't pigeonhole this guy. He's an odd mix of things, not to mention coming from a culture she knows nothing about.

They walk down to the Inner Harbour, where a crowd has gathered in a fidgety clump around one of the buskers. Inching their way in, Kennedy sees it's Silver Man. He's been here every summer since Kennedy arrived. Any exposed skin is a shimmering silver, like the tin man in *The Wizard of Oz*, except he wears a man's suit that's been spray-painted silver, a silver hat and silver sneakers. He's totally frozen, a human statue, and mirrored silver sunglasses hide his eyes.

"You have to see Silver Man," says Kennedy to Colin, boldly taking his arm and pulling him through the crowd to stand up near the front. "Keep watching," she whispers. "He only moves when somebody puts money in his box."

They wait, Colin jiggling one restless leg until suddenly Elliot steps out of the crowd and drops a coin in the box. Quick and precise hands fold across the front and back of his waist as Silver Man abruptly bows his thanks. He's down and up and back into a new frozen position in a matter of seconds.

Kennedy smiles up at Colin, who smiles back. Elliot comes to stand beside them.

"You make it too easy for him," says Colin. "He a friend of yours, maybe? Got a bun under that hat?"

Elliot sighs as if he's holding his tongue. Then Colin is stepping toward Silver Man.

Sarina knocks Kennedy's arm. "What's he up to?"

Colin bends over the money box at Silver Man's feet, and instead of putting money in, lifts out a fiver. A gasp trips around the audience. Then, holding it level with the frozen silver face, Colin slowly crumples the bill into his fist. He makes as if to walk away and Silver Man follows, gliding along on his feet, robotlike, his arms following suit. "Ooh," rises from the crowd.

Colin stops and turns just as Silver Man stops. Colin takes the bill and dangles it alongside the busker's stiff palm, which is laid open as if prepared to shake hands. When he tickles Silver Man's palm with the fiver, the audience swells with laughter. Colin's mischievous smile is reflected in Silver Man's sunglasses. Elliot, who's standing beside Kennedy, turns and leaves. She stares after him but then Sarina tugs at her shirt.

"Watch," she says excitedly.

So slowly it is almost imperceptible, Silver Man is closing his hand around the bill. But just before his silver fingers make contact, Colin pulls it up in the air and then walks around Silver Man to the money box and drops it in. Instead of landing in the box, it catches the air and just misses. The audience laughs. Colin does a bow mirroring Silver Man's bow and exits. A little boy, maybe six or seven, a worried expression on his face, rushes to retrieve the bill and puts it in the box. The audience bursts into applause as Silver Man shakes a robotic finger toward Colin and then holds out a frozen hand to the little boy for a shake.

"You're so bad," Sarina teases Colin.

"Just hoping to impress you girls," he says, then gives Kennedy's arm a squeeze. "I'll be right back."

"Sure," she says and watches him get swallowed up by people and disappear.

"Where's he going?" asks Sarina.

"He didn't say." Kennedy strains to pick out his blond head moving through the crowd. "Said he'll be right back, though. Maybe he's gone to find Elliot."

"Yeah, and where did Elliot go?"

"I'm right here," he says, suddenly behind them. "A fire juggler is just starting up down the way. Shall we watch him?"

"Colin just left," Kennedy says. "I thought maybe he went to find you."

He looks at her with one cockeyed brow as if she's joking. "We'll be lucky if we see him again today." Kennedy can't think why Elliot would say that.

"He said he'd be right back. Maybe we should wait here."

"He'll find us if and when he wants to," says Elliot. "Come on."

Is he jealous of Colin? wonders Kennedy. Or embarrassed by Colin one-upping him with Silver Man? Maybe he's mad because of that jab about the busker having a bun under his hat. That remark was pretty low, but then Elliot's a prickly sort. Reluctantly she follows him and Sarina. The Inner Harbour's not that big a place, she tells herself. Colin will find them. She watches Elliot's long hair shiver along his back as he walks. She's always wanted straight hair. He's a very unbald eagle, she jokes to herself.

The juggler's act lasts a full forty minutes and still no Colin. Kennedy hopes he's not busy looking for them. Elliot has gone up to talk to the juggler as if he knows him. He says something that makes the juggler laugh, then drops some money into his collection hat. Kennedy feels a little guilty for not giving up some of her five, but that's all she has for lunch. Elliot sees her and waves her over, his hand like a command.

"He's awfully bossy," says Kennedy, suddenly irritable. "Conceited, too."

"Who?" asks Sarina.

"This Elliot guy."

"His father drives a cab, how conceited can he be?" says Sarina, and Kennedy looks at her in surprise.

"His father *owns* a cab company," she corrects. "And apparently Elliot's really smart and got all sorts of scholarships to attend university." She doesn't know why she's defending him.

"Doesn't it seem like the Chinese kids and East Indian kids are always getting better grades than the Canadian kids?" says Sarina offhandedly.

"They're just as Canadian as we are," Kennedy says.

"You know what I mean." Sarina tries to explain it better. "I just wonder sometimes if we more 'privileged types,'" her fingers pump quotation marks into the air, "take our lives for granted and so don't try as hard."

"I know what you mean," Kennedy has to agree. "Whenever Liam or I complain about material stuff, Dad says he's going to move us to the third world."

"Why is it called the third and first world? And what happened to second place?"

"I've no idea."

"Of course, there's Miko," says Sarina. "She doesn't kill herself studying."

"No, but her parents made her do all that extra Kumon math in grade school."

"True. And she has a tutor come exam time."

They make their way over to where Elliot is now standing, weirdly still, focused on the seaplane about to take off from the harbour. It churns up the water with an ear-piercing buzz as it skims ahead, picking up speed, and finally lifts into the air.

"I'm hungry," says Sarina as the noise fades.

"Let's go to Zombie's," suggests Kennedy. "Colin knew we wanted to eat there."

"It's no longer called Zombie's," corrects Elliot, sounding like a schoolteacher.

Kennedy catches Sarina's eye.

"Does it still have good pizza?" asks Sarina.

"Nothing's really changed except the name," he answers.

"Whatever," says Kennedy, looking around again for Colin.

"Don't bother," says Elliot as if reading her mind. "He's likely gone for the day."

PAIN #18: KNOW-IT-ALLS

How can anybody be sure of anything when there's like a million variables at all times?

"I liked the name Zombie's," says Sarina. "What did they change it to?"

"You'll see," says Elliot, gesturing for them to go ahead of him on the crowded sidewalk.

How gentleman-like, mocks Kennedy, resenting his superior tone.

The painted sign above the open door shows an array of phallus-shaped vegetables and fruit.

"Peckerheads?" Kennedy and Sarina read together, then look at each other and break up laughing. Elliot says nothing, just continues on through the open door. The girls follow as soon as they can stand up straight again. Inside, Peckerheads has the same red and black walls as Zombie's, even the pizza smell in the air is the same.

"Hey, Elliot," says the guy behind the counter. His head is shaved to a shine, he has sinister black eyebrows and every possible part of his face is pierced with little gold rings threaded with a single black bead.

"Milo," returns Elliot, "how's it going?"

Kennedy tries not to be impressed that nerdy Elliot knows this scary-looking guy named Milo. Because of the taxi business, she imagines. Maybe Elliot's a driver for his dad's company and spends time in here between customers.

"These are my friends, Kennedy and Sarina," says Elliot.

Instead of saying hi to her and Sarina, the pierced guy says "sure" to Elliot, and Kennedy catches sight of a stud the size of a ball bearing in the centre of his tongue. Ouch, she thinks, shuddering. She can't imagine why people do that. Willow's been saying Graham wants her to get a tongue stud. Kennedy didn't ask why and doesn't want to know.

"I've got pepperoni with red peckers or mango and banana peckers," Milo reels off with a bored face.

Kennedy can't help but turn to Sarina and laugh girlishly. She'd never act so silly if Colin were here, but she doesn't really care what Elliot thinks.

"Pepperoni okay, girls?" says Elliot, looking impatient.

"Yeah, sure," giggles Sarina, fishing money out of her purse. "I'll have a Sprite too."

"We *are* capable of deciding for ourselves," Kennedy says to Elliot as she slips past him and up to the counter next to Sarina.

"Hawaiian for me, please," says Kennedy, "and an Orange Crush."

"It's okay," says Milo, waving off Sarina's ten-dollar bill. "It's on the house."

Kennedy looks at Elliot.

"I fix their computer," he says with a shrug.

They take their food outside to sit in Bastion Square, where a band of musicians are playing exotic percussive instruments. Their quick, sunny music seems a perfect reflection of the weather's airy brightness, thinks Kennedy.

"Great sound," she says, settling on a step, and Elliot smiles at her as if in approval.

One point for me, she thinks.

"Wonder where they're from?" says Sarina.

"Mexico, maybe," says Kennedy.

"They're from Ecuador," Elliot says, with too much authority. Kennedy can't look at him.

She cranes her neck to scan up and down the square for Colin, then takes a sip of pop.

"Pepperoni and red peckers," whispers Sarina in Kennedy's ear and Kennedy chokes on her drink.

At the outdoor café on the corner, a woman laughs loudly, a goofy hiccuping type of laugh that sounds just like her mom's. She looks over, relieved to see it's a stranger. A few days ago it *was* her mom, laughing in a café up on Government Street. Kennedy and Miko had bused down to the Bay Centre looking for bathing suits on sale. Mom was having lunch with her new theatre friends, the woman from the playground and some man. The man was good-looking for his age and had expensive-looking sunglasses parked on top of his head. His dark hair, probably dyed, was just the slightest bit grey at his temples. Kennedy remembers thinking how much younger Dad would look if he dyed his hair. The guy's black shirt was open at the collar and a gold chain glittered around his neck. She hoped this was a sign he was gay. She could never, in a million years, imagine Dad wearing a necklace. She couldn't bring herself to go say hi, but knew that if she were alone, she would have spied on them, maybe even followed them back to the theatre. Later Kennedy told her mom she had seen her having lunch downtown.

"Oh yeah, we were on break."

"Was the man with you ... the director?" Kennedy had asked, watching closely for a reaction.

"Yes, David. Nice guy. Very funny."

Kennedy shrugged. "Is he gay?" she asked.

Mom looked at her funny. "I don't think so. Why?"

"Just curious." Kennedy wanted to ask if he was married but knew it would sound even more weird so dropped it.

"I wonder if having a big stud in your mouth like Milo lessens your appetite," says Sarina. "Like sucking on a mint all the time."

"If only they made flavoured ones," says Kennedy.

"I could never do it." Sarina cringes. "It must hurt like crazy. I thought I'd faint when I got my ears done. Could hear the different layers of flesh ripping as they punched it through."

"I read somewhere," says Kennedy, "that there's two muscles and one major vein that run through the middle of your tongue and that the piercing has to miss all three or you can die."

She is unable to tell by Elliot's silence and averted eyes if he's even listening. She wonders if he finds the conversation beneath him.

"Some people are whacked," says Sarina and bites into her pizza.

Kennedy is watching the xylophone player when she sees Colin trotting down Bastion Square toward them.

"Colin," Kennedy calls and waves. She tries to give Elliot a "see, you were wrong" look, but he won't look her way.

"Found you," he says, squeezing himself a seat between her and Sarina. "Mmm ... pizza."

He lifts Kennedy's pizza hand up to his mouth and takes a bite while looking at her with those eyes. She doesn't look away and somehow this feels as intimate as if he'd kissed her.

"So good," he says, and wipes his mouth with the back of his hand.

"Have the rest," says Kennedy, wanting to please him. "I'm finished."

"You sure?"

"I'd just throw it away."

"Can't let that happen."

Kennedy catches Elliot staring at her. He quickly looks away. What sort of judgement is he passing now?

"So where were you?" asks Sarina.

"Scored some of your famous B.C. bud," he says with a wink. "To give our afternoon more ... dimension. I bought it from some blue-haired chick outside of McDonald's."

"She has pretty clean stuff, meaning it isn't dusted, but she overcharges," says Elliot.

Colin laughs at him. "Good one, Narwhal. So, ladies, do you care to join me in a," he holds two fingers to his lips, "after this lovely pizza?"

Sarina and Kennedy exchange looks. Despite her own mother's proclivities, or maybe because of them, Kennedy has never smoked weed before, or anything else for that matter, and knows Sarina hasn't either. She's relieved by what Elliot just said about this stuff being pretty clean, though she's no idea what being dusted means. She's been to enough drug talks at school to know that what you think you're getting from a dealer is not always what it actually is.

"We've never gotten high before," says Sarina, being that much harder to embarrass than Kennedy.

Colin's face seems to light up with this admission. "Your first time, eh?" he says, lifting his eyebrows suggestively.

Kennedy feels herself blush. Sarina laughs and gives his shoulder a playful shove.

"How about the Narwhal? Ever been stoned there, Elliot?"

"Not today," is all he says, his eyes giving away nothing.

"Good, then you can take care of the rest of us, eh Sahib? So, ladies?" Colin asks again.

"Sure," Sarina says, glancing at Kennedy.

"First time for everything," says Kennedy.

On the periphery of Beacon Hill Park, and inside a dense grove of trees, Colin rolls a joint with the same brand of papers that Kennedy found in the tin on her kitchen shelf. She tries to picture her mother sprinkling dry green leaves down the center of a paper, rolling it up and licking it closed. For the final step, Colin drags the whole torpedo-shaped joint through his wetted lips.

"Gross," says Sarina. "We're supposed to smoke that now?"

Looking intent on his task, Colin ignores her and fishes in his pocket for matches.

Kennedy leans over to Sarina's ear. "Pecker-joint," she whispers, and they both burst out laughing.

"Whispering is impolite," says Colin, puffing on the joint to get it started. He finishes with a large inhale, then passes it to Kennedy. "Here," he says, holding his breath.

She takes it and holds it up to her lips, feeling the moistness where Colin's lips have been. She drags on the joint and a stinging heat hits her virgin lungs. She copies Colin, holding the smoke in, but her eyes fill with water and she coughs violently.

"Ow," she says, holding her chest. "Hurts." She passes the joint to Sarina.

"Here," says Elliot, handing her the bottle of Evian he'd got at Peckerheads.

"Takes getting used to," Colin says. "Seasoned lungs here." He beats his chest with two fists and does a Tarzan yell.

Kennedy coughs and laughs at the same time. She drinks some of Elliot's water and hands it back with a "thanks." Elliot surprises her by catching her eye and smiling softly. Impossible to tell what that guy's thinking, she says to herself.

"Hey, did you know Evian spelled backwards is 'naïve'?" says Colin. "I think some French fellow is laughing all the way to the bank."

Sarina has taken a more tentative drag and only hiccups a little cough. She waves off Elliot's offer of water and holds the joint out to Colin.

"I'll have one hit," says Elliot, carefully removing it from Sarina's fingers.

"All right, Elliot!" cheers Colin. "But who's going to take care of us now?" His eyebrows knit together over his eyes and his beautiful lips pout.

Elliot draws deeply, smoking with the same casual ease with which he does everything. It definitely looks as if he's done it before. He doesn't cough, but lets the smoke drift lazily from his mouth. Kennedy's eyes trace the pronounced lines of his cheekbones and she muses how his colouring makes his lips look outlined in pencil — the way Willow does her lips. Nice lips, she thinks, but nothing like Colin's.

They pass the joint around a couple more times, Elliot keeping his word and sticking to the one puff. Kennedy's eyes have started buzzing, as if they're plugged into a steady stream of low-voltage electricity. Now the silence is permeated by a loud humming that reminds her of the cicadas back east. No, she thinks, it's just the frequency the air's vibrating at. Why hadn't she noticed that sound before? Maybe she just never listened hard enough. She wonders if the others hear it.

"So, how does it feel?" Colin's voice shatters her thought.

His eyes look as if they're squinting. Kennedy is unsure whether she can talk right now. By the tight feel of her cheek muscles, she realizes she's smiling.

"All prickly," says Sarina, glancing around the circle.

"Congratulations," Colin says. "You're stoned." Now he's talking really slow.

"And don't worry, it's all temporary," adds Elliot, talking even slower.

Kennedy looks at Elliot to try and figure out exactly what he means by this. Being high is temporary, or life in general?

"Whatever you say, Elliot," says Colin.

It feels as if nobody says anything for an awfully long time until Sarina pipes up in a weirdly high-pitched, cartoon mouse voice, "Can I braid your hair?"

She says this to Elliot.

He nods, drags the elastic from his ponytail and turns his back to her.

"It's so soft," Sarina mumbles. "Smells like spice."

"My mother's cooking."

Watching Sarina work the long dark strands, Kennedy

thinks she can feel just what her friend's hands are feeling. Let me touch, Kennedy tries to say, reaching for his hair, but no words come out. Elliot's hair feels like cat fur and satin woven together, she thinks, letting the black hair slide through her fingers.

"Nice," she manages to mumble and reluctantly removes her hand.

Sarina arranges herself behind Elliot and now both their backs are turned. Kennedy feels startlingly alone with Colin, as if a soundproof glass dome has descended over the two of them.

"Kennedy, would you mind scratching my back?" Colin's musical voice seems to penetrate right through her skull.

Before she even answers, he's taken off his shirt and is scooting toward her.

"Okay," she says and wonders if her voice is as loud as it sounds in her head.

She takes her nails to his smooth, muscled skin, warm under her palm.

"Ooh, good," he mumbles. "A little harder."

She scratches harder and her nails leave white lines behind. The lines turn red and she's afraid she might be hurting him. His soft groans sound only pleasurable, so she continues.

"Lower," he says and he bends forward.

His pants pull low off his back and Kennedy shyly takes her nails along the bumpy imprint left by the elastic waist of his boxers. After an unknowable length of time, he sits up and turns to her.

"My back thanks you," he says, reaching one hand to her face.

Like some sort of slow-motion dream, his eyes close and his face comes at hers and then he's kissing her, forcing her lips apart with his tongue. She's as surprised as she is amazed. She's just met this guy, doesn't really know anything about him, yet the sensation is overpowering and she closes her eyes and kisses him back. A real kiss, a stronger, more full-bodied kiss than she's ever had. She can taste the nicotine and pot in his mouth, the ham from the pizza. She's aware of the slight roughness above his lip. She's kissing a man's mouth. Surrendering to the sensations of his roaming tongue, she feels a sudden firm hand on her breast.

"Oh," she blurts, startled, as she pulls her mouth from his. She must have said it louder than she meant to because Elliot and Sarina have turned around.

"What?" asks Elliot, sounding concerned, fatherly.

Colin has pulled away and is fiddling with a leaf on the ground.

"Oh, nothing," Kennedy says, confused. "Just ... just a kink in my neck."

She quickly reaches her hand to her neck and Colin gives her a conspiratorial smile. She smiles back, hoping he's not mad at her. It was neat, it was great, just a little fast for her. She was surprised, is all. He picks up his shirt and his muscled chest with its diamond of curls disappears underneath.

"Look at my braid," says Sarina, holding Elliot's tail of hair in her hands. "I braided it in three braids and then braided the braids together. Ooh, did that sound funny?"

Colin starts laughing, a loose, guffawing laugh that sets the rest of them laughing too, even Elliot. They're laughing so hard they're holding their stomachs. Kennedy's cheeks ache from smiling so hard. She laughs partly from what Sarina said, partly from nerves and partly because of the amazing harmonic sound of their laughter. Colin's the bass tenor, Elliot the tenor, Kennedy the alto and Sarina the soprano. Beautiful. The universe suddenly seems to make perfect musical sense.

When they finally calm down, Elliot suggests they walk around. "Maybe get an ice cream."

"Oh, yeah," says Sarina.

"Let's," seconds Kennedy. Having forgone half her pizza slice, she's still hungry and ice cream sounds like the absolute best thing in the entire world right now.

They all end up with double-sized chocolate-and-vanilla twists from the Beacon Drive-In. The soft ice cream tastes like cool heaven on Kennedy's tongue. Cones in hand, they walk back toward the harbour. Sarina says she wants to window shop, Elliot says he should check in on a few people and Colin wants to wander about on his own. Kennedy is insecure at the thought of them breaking apart, would prefer if they all stayed together, especially her and Colin, but doesn't say anything.

They agree to meet back at the cab in an hour's time, at seven-thirty, and then move off in their different directions. Kennedy admires Colin's backside as he strides away, then has to run to catch up to Sarina, who's gone ahead without her. Sarina seems to know exactly where she wants to go. Besides the Bay Centre, Kennedy doesn't know

Victoria's downtown stores. They head through an alley
to a side street lined with funky shops with smudged
windows.

"Sarina, I have to tell you something."

"What is it?"

"Colin and I made out back in the park."

"Get out, really?"

"I'm serious. And then he put his hand on my boob
and I was so shocked I kinda screamed."

"That's what that was. Hey, Kennedy's got a new
boyfriend," Sarina chants. "She's in the big leagues now.
Poor Jordan."

"Yeah, I'm terrible, aren't I?"

"No."

Kennedy pauses. "It might have just been because he
was high," she says, fishing for Sarina's opinion.

"No, I can tell he likes you. He looks at you, you know,
that way."

"What way?" Despite sore cheek muscles, Kennedy smiles.

"Like you're ice cream," says Sarina. "And he wants to
lick you all over." She leans over and licks Kennedy's arm.

"You're joking."

"Well, *he's* not," she says, walking into a gift store.

Kennedy grabs her arm. "Hey, don't tell anyone. I'd feel
terrible if Jordan found out."

Sarina mimes zipping her lips.

Inside the store, Kennedy's thoughts are swimming.
What about Jordan? And what about tonight, later at
home, with Colin sleeping so close by?

On the store shelves, the littlest things draw Kennedy's
eye — coloured plastic bracelets, an angel made from

straw, a carved-crystal chicken. She tries to picture exactly how these things got made, her mind a jumble of hands and machines. Senses becomes magnified when you're high, she thinks, noticing how her focus has shifted from total absorption in the smooth planes of the glass chicken to total absorption in the sound of a passing car, then to an itch on her scalp and now to the red of these candles. It's as if she can experience only one sense perception at a time, however briefly. Maybe, she wonders, our minds are so speedy that we think we're experiencing all our senses at once, but in reality it's one after another in rapid-fire succession. And what about when we're thinking thoughts? Are we still sensing? Or are thoughts another sense?

"My mother would love this," says Sarina, snapping Kennedy out of her reverie.

"What?" she asks, relieved to be rescued from what seemed to be endless doorways of thought.

"This silver and onyx bracelet," says Sarina. "Mom has earrings almost just like it."

"Too bad we can't get your dad to buy it. As a romantic present."

"Would have to be with her money." Sarina sounds sad again.

"Sorry to bring it up. That was stupid of me," Kennedy apologizes.

"I'm going to have to get used to it."

Kennedy's thoughts veer to her own parents. If divorce could happen to Sarina's parents, it could happen to any-one's. Dad has a thing about honesty. If he found out Mom cheated on him, he'd probably divorce her on the spot. Maybe, thinks Kennedy, if Dad was more romantic and took Mom out to lunch on Government Street, bought her presents for no occasion — flowers, a box of Rogers' chocolates. Kennedy pictures a dozen red roses — no, eleven red and one white, lying on her mom's pillow. No card, no explanation. Just roses. That would be so romantic. Mom would love it. Or maybe the two of them could go away for a weekend. That's supposed to be good. They could go to Hornby Island — Mom loves Hornby — and Kennedy would offer to babysit.

She scans the display case full of silver and gold bracelets inlaid with semi-precious stones. Mom would love that gold one with the tiger's eye. Oh yes, the roses could be held together with a bracelet instead of ribbon. Imagine. She could buy the bracelet and Dad could give it to Mom. She could tell him that she overheard Mom talking on the phone, saying that she wasn't sure he loved her anymore. He'd be sad to hear it but it would sure make him more attentive. Maybe, thinks Kennedy, she could even talk him into dyeing his hair.

"How much is that one?" Kennedy asks the lady behind the counter.

"Two hundred and twenty dollars."

Forget the bracelet. She'll use a nice ribbon.

"Hey," calls Sarina. "Like this hat on me?"

At seven-thirty, Kennedy and Sarina head back to Elliot's cab. The pot's pretty well worn off, leaving a feeling in Kennedy's head of being filled with dust. Elliot's sitting on the hood of his car, staring out over the harbour, his hair still woven in its thick triple braid. Colin's nowhere to be seen.

"Hi," he says as they come around the car.

"No Colin?" asks Kennedy, her stomach fluttering at the thought of him.

"We'll wait another ten or so and then he can find his way."

"We can't just leave him."

"He's a big boy, Kennedy," says Elliot.

That serene-eyed stare of Elliot's makes Kennedy feel exposed and self-conscious. She looks away.

Sarina pulls the bucket hat she bought out of its bag and tries it on. "You like?" she says to Elliot and proceeds to model it, slinking up and down the sidewalk while sucking in her cheeks. Kennedy laughs, happy to see Sarina joking around.

They wait ten minutes and still no Colin.

"Shall we go?" says Elliot, hopping off the car hood.

"Just five more minutes?" pleads Kennedy, and he replants himself on the car.

Five minutes pass and still no sign of Colin. Kennedy's feeling a little like she's been dumped.

"Let's go," says Sarina. "Like Elliot says, he'll find his way." She strokes Kennedy's back, knowing she's disappointed.

"Sure, let's."

Elliot says nothing, just gets in the car.

Sarina gets in the back and Kennedy, feeling weird about Elliot being alone in the front taxiing them home, climbs into the passenger seat. "Mind if I sit up front?" she asks Elliot.

"No," he answers without looking at her.

Gee, she thought she was doing him a favour.

They pull away from the taxi stand and into the light evening traffic. The breeze through the open windows is summer perfect and Kennedy wishes she were in the back seat with Colin's arm around her shoulder, the radio on, their thighs pressed together. Should she ask Elliot to turn the radio on? Opera would be fine with her.

"So you're at Lambrick?" says Elliot.

"Yeah, Sarina and I are going into grade ten."

"They have great sports teams."

"Yeah, both the boys' and girls' senior soccer and basketball teams went to the provincials this year. Boys won both. Girls came third in soccer and second in basketball." He probably already knows this, but appears to be listening so intently that she felt a need to fill out her answer. "And you graduated from where?" It's only polite to ask him back.

"Claremont."

"Oh, they're supposed to have one of the best art programs in the city."

"Yeah, I really enjoyed the poetry courses."

Kennedy is surprised to hear these words from a guy's lips. "You like poetry?"

"The contemporary stuff. And writing's a nice way to get things off your chest."

Kennedy looks over. He's perfectly serious. She doesn't know how to respond.

"But I went there for the music," he continues. "I play cello and viola."

"That's great," Kennedy says and means it. "I play a little piano."

"Kennedy has a great voice too," Sarina pipes up.

Elliot looks over at Kennedy with those sincere eyes of his.

"But she hates it when I mention it."

"Yes, I do, *Sarina*."

"To be able to sing is a gift," he says simply. "What sort of music do you like?"

"Uh, all sorts, really. Rock, opera, pop, choir music."

"The Victoria Choir is excellent. Ever heard them sing?" Elliot asks.

"No, I haven't." It's weird to Kennedy to be having such an "adult" conversation with a teenage guy.

"You should. They do Handel's *Messiah* every Christmas. It's brilliant."

"Really?" says Kennedy, excitedly. "We used to go hear the *Messiah* every year in Fredericton. My aunt sang in the choir. I'd never fail to fly in my dreams after that concert."

Elliot has stopped talking and is just smiling at the road ahead of him. Paranoid that she might have just sounded really childish, Kennedy changes the subject.

"Can I ask you a computer question?"

"Sure."

"Oh, yeah, tell him about Zak," says Sarina.

"Zak?" asks Elliot.

"Some pervert on MSN," says Sarina.

"We don't know that," Kennedy says to Sarina. "But there is this guy suddenly on MSN who nobody knows and he's asking girls how old they are and where they live and stuff."

Elliot just listens.

"But *my* question is whether people can be listening in without you knowing it?"

"MSN is what's called an open line and, yes, anybody can listen in if they know how."

"On private conversations?" asks Sarina.

"Sure. So be careful who you slander."

"It sounds like those old party-line phones," says Kennedy.

"Pretty much. And there are people known as cyberstalkers who harass and even threaten people."

"So Liam didn't make up that word."

"Liam?"

"My brother. He tends to make up words."

"Is there a way to trace this Zak guy?" asks Sarina.

"Not really," says Elliot. "There's too many ways to cover your tracks. Even the police don't have a proper tracking system."

"Hey, Kennedy," says Sarina, leaning forward. "We should try and smoke out this Zak guy. If he's really listening to our conversations, we could plan on MSN to meet someplace at a specific time and then a second place and see if the same guy shows up at both places."

"That's a cool idea," says Kennedy.

"I wouldn't directly engage him online if I were you," says Elliot.

"Right." Kennedy turns to Sarina. "We don't talk to him, we only plant the messages and then keep an eye out for him."

"We'll be like private detectives," says Sarina. "Smoke him out, then alert the police."

"You should be careful," says Elliot, sounding fatherly again. "Stuff happens."

Sarina's place is on the way, so Elliot drops her off first. He never did put on the radio and, on the short drive to Kennedy's house, the silence in the car feels oddly expectant.

"It was fun today," she says as they pull into the driveway. "Thanks a lot for driving."

"No problem, it was nice meeting you both. And interesting seeing Colin again," he adds with a funny little smile.

"Bye," she says, getting out of the car.

He waits there until she's safely inside. She appreciates the gesture. Her father always waits for her friends, a consideration she's proud of. Stepping inside, she smells cigarette smoke in the air. Old or new, she wonders, hurrying to the rec room. Maybe somehow he got here before us, thinks Kennedy, her heart beating a little faster. No one is in the rec room. As she heads upstairs, she hears machine-gun fire coming from the living room.

"Better get a life, Manny," Liam is saying. "'Cause you've just lost this one." His tone changes to a kind of singsong rap. "Ooh ... I think I'm feeling sexy. I think, I feel, I think, I feel, I think I am a sexy thing who's going to whup your ass."

"Hi, Liam," says Kennedy.

"It's my sister, Ken-ne-dy," he raps. "She's tall, she's sexy, I think I'll whup her ass."

"Stop that, please. Where is everyone?"

"It's only you and me, K-Dot, against the world. The rest have been taken by helicopter to Spider Island." He reaches into his pants pocket. "Left us a twenty for pizza."

"Pizza. Did Colin come home?"

"No-see-um big boyum. You like the big boyum, do yum?"

Kennedy grabs the twenty out of his hands. The adults and Tory must have gone out to dinner, she figures, and Colin never made it home.

"Let's order Chinese instead," says Kennedy.

"No way, pizza," says Liam.

"Come on, I had pizza for lunch. You like the sweet and sour pork."

"Okay. And spring rolls. And those dumpling things."

"Fine, but I have to see how much it all costs," says Kennedy, gazing out the window to the street.

"Where are you, big boyum?" she whispers to the glass. "And what did this afternoon mean?"

14

PAIN #19: THAT SOUND

Kennedy has awoken to an obnoxious beeping. Did she accidentally set the alarm? The repetitive blare is getting louder and louder. Oh, it's the recycling truck, thinks Kennedy, sounding its stupid warning signal as it backs up. Does it really have to be that loud? Are there that many deaf people in the world?

She pulls the sides of the pillow over her ears. She has yet to open her eyes, knowing that once that happens, going back to sleep is out of the question. She lies there, hoping to drift off again, but her eyes are wide awake beneath their lids. She gives in and looks at the clock — only eight. Closes her eyes again. Well, she *was* in bed by eleven. Read for half an hour all about Elizabeth running into Mr. Darcy on her morning constitutional. Mr. Darcy had been waiting for her, to give her a letter he'd written explaining the crimes she'd accused him of. The letter mainly discussed his dealings with Wickham. Mr. Wickham, apparently, was a cad who had not only squandered the money left him by Mr. Darcy's father, but had once seduced

Mr. Darcy's sister, Georgiana, into believing she was in love with him and then made plans for a secret elopement. Georgiana was only fifteen at the time. Mr. Darcy had found out about the intended elopement and banished Wickham from his association. Imagine, eloping at fifteen, thinks Kennedy. Of course, if Mr. Wickham were as gorgeous as Colin ...

Kennedy suddenly remembers him coming home late last night and the noises in the rec room that woke her up. It was Judith's voice, scolding Colin about smoking in the house. Then her voice went more muffled before rising again, tight and angry-sounding. She said something about "behaving or he can go right back to face things at home." Kennedy was too sleepy to make sense of it then, but now she wonders what that could have meant. What did Colin have to face at home?

She doesn't want to get out of bed but has to pee something fierce. Chinese food always makes her thirsty and she had three glasses of water before bed. Putting on her robe, she leaves her glasses in her pocket, in case Colin's awake, and quietly opens her door. The rec room smells terrible. Like dead mouse.

She manoeuvres blind across the room, squinting to see Colin lying on top of his covers, his jeans still on, T-shirt off, his mouth slung open. He's snoring a soft, snuffly snore as though his nose is stopped up. She fears the dead rodent smell is coming from his mouth. She pictures kissing him yesterday and can't connect this mouth with that one. He looks positively cemented in sleep. She clears her throat loudly. No reaction. Then she does it again, louder. His snores don't miss a beat. She puts on her glasses. It would take an army of beeping trucks to wake him up.

Upstairs, Mom and Dad are making coffee while Tory draws with fat markers at the kitchen table. Judith is nowhere to be seen. Perhaps after waiting up for Colin last night, she's sleeping in too.

"Smell my markers, Kendy," demands Tory.

"Good morning, Kennedy," says Dad.

"Morning."

"The brown one smells just like chocolate milk. Come see."

Bending over the table, Tory holds the brown marker up to Kennedy's nose and accidentally pokes her with it.

"Ow."

"Sorry, Kendy," she giggles.

"Is it on me?" asks Kennedy, rubbing her nose on the back of her hand. She looks at the brown smear across her knuckles.

"Now you have a doggy nose," says Tory. "A chocolate milk doggy nose."

"Thanks a lot." Kennedy heads to the sink to wash it off.

"I'm making pancakes for Tory. Want one?" asks her dad.

"Letter pancakes," says Tory. "A "v" for Victoria and a "t" for Tory."

Kennedy can remember Dad doing the same for her and Liam once upon a time. Her "k" was always the hardest one to make, its legs more often than not, running together and turning it into a "y."

"No thanks, I'll just have cereal."

"Have a piece of fruit too, please," says Mom. "The nectarines need eating."

Mom and her fruit, thinks Kennedy. Her mom is emptying the dishwasher. Kennedy is glad to see her dressed in one of her old summer dresses, a nice loose one that doesn't show any curves or belly skin. She has the sudden urge to tell her about smoking pot for the first time. They could compare notes. But this mom here and the one who smokes pot on the sly and hangs at cafés seem like two vastly different people.

"Where's Liam?" Kennedy asks, out of habit, and realizes she still feels pretty fuzzy-brained from yesterday.

"Sam's," says Mom.

"And how's it going with Judith?" she asks in a quieter voice.

Mom teeters her palm in the air in the "so-so" sign and Dad pulls a face. He obviously thinks Judith's a bit off too.

"Judith's changed a lot," says Mom. "She's not a very happy woman."

At least Colin makes up for his weird mother, thinks Kennedy.

Over one mushy, overripe nectarine and a bowl of Just Right, Kennedy reads about Elizabeth's reaction to Mr. Darcy's letter. Elizabeth is shocked to learn about Mr. Wickham's dishonourable character and understands now that she was mistaken to believe in Wickham's all-too-easy manner. Still, Elizabeth cannot forgive Mr. Darcy for interfering with Mr. Bingley's feelings for her sister Jane. He claims he was trying to protect his friend from the stigma of marrying beneath him.

When Elizabeth shared with Jane the deceits of Mr. Wickham, together they decided to keep the truth about Wickham to themselves. Mr. Darcy, they reasoned, would not want the story of his sister's near elopement to get out.

"*Poor Wickham,*" says Jane; "*there is such an expression of goodness in his countenance! Such openness and gentleness in his manner.*"

"*One has got all the goodness,*" replies Elizabeth, "*and the other all the appearance of it.*"

After breakfast, Kennedy heads to the computer. Sarina's rarely awake before noon, so Kennedy's surprised to find her online this early.

hey sar, wuz up?

hi ken, slept horribly las night. pot? couldn't stop thinking about dad movin out. shit. i jus wan to run away n then com back n it be ok again

it sucks. have u talked to ur parents about it?

not yet

get them to spell out what happened between them. u deserve 2 know

Kennedy feels like a hypocrite. She should take her own advice and ask Mom a few questions of her own.

ur right. did i ever tell u, ur a genius?

lol

The word "genius" brings Elliot to mind. He's weird enough to be some sort of genius. What kind of teenager does computer work for restaurants anyway?

*colin came home super late last night. think he ws drunk.
his mom ws really mad. i'll be nervous to talk to hm after
yesterday. smokin ws kinda fun but my head feels full of
smoke this morning*

*yea, i feel stupid today. but whats new? much better than
a hangover tho. don't worry bout colin, just be yourself. if
thats not enough thn screw him, metaphorically speaking
that is. lol*

That's the first time Sarina's mentioned anything about
getting hammered, thinks Kennedy, before noticing the
message symbol blinking. She moves the mouse down to
check who's logging on.

zak

Oh shit. Kennedy clicks up the message.

*hi ken, that's short for a girl's name isn't it? you r a girl
right? or should i say a young woman?*

Ick. She clicks off without responding.

sar, gotta go. Call u on ur cell.

ok.

Kennedy goes downstairs to call Sarina. In the rec room,
Colin is now snoring like a purring cat. A very large cat,
that is. She opens a window to let in some fresh air.
He groans and rolls onto his side. A curl of hair drops over
one eye. Too cute, she thinks, wanting but not daring to
brush it back off his face.

"Sarina?"

"Yeah. Why did you get offline so fast?"

"Zak sent me a message."

"No way, what was it?"

"Oh, he's gross. Asked if I was a young woman."

"He's a pervert, all right. Let's plan to meet somewhere and see if he shows up."

"If we met at some secluded place, like Mount Doug beach, then we could tell right away," says Kennedy. "Of course, we should probably have more people around, just in case he's dangerous."

"Is Miko still in town?"

"No, she left for Ontario. Niagara Falls. I think there's some Judy Garland tribute happening at the Stratford Festival."

"Get your boyfriend Colin to come with us."

"He's hardly my boyfriend. For all I know about him, he might be engaged." Kennedy hears Judith's angry voice — *go back and face things at home.* "Let's plan to meet somewhere more public first. Say the playground at Majestic Park. There's always lots of people around, so that would be safe. We could meet there this afternoon and then maybe plan another meeting at Video Stop tonight. I haven't seen the last Harry Potter since it came out on DVD."

"Yeah, sure. Harry's getting seriously cute. And I need things to take my mind off my screwed-up family."

Now that she's talking about things, Sarina sounds so much better, thinks Kennedy.

"Sometimes splitting up is the sane thing to do for a while."

"Maybe," says Sarina. "But, you know, I never saw them fight or anything. So it's weird, like it just happened really gradually. Like they just slowly drifted apart into these separate lives. Sorry to keep on about it," says Sarina.

"No, it's good."

"Thanks. But yeah, let's meet at Majestic and Video Stop today, and tomorrow see if Colin and our friends want to go to the beach. We could have a fire, roast wieners, make s'mores."

"Sounds great. Talk to you on MSN. And hey, let's take our tennis rackets to Majestic."

"Fun. We haven't played tennis for ages."

15

The playground at Majestic is noisy with screaming kids and scolding parents. Two kids are already playing on the single tennis court, so Sarina and Kennedy place their rackets inside the fence to claim the court next and go have a swing on the swings. They keep an eye out for suspicious-looking guys over at the baseball diamond or hanging around the bus stop. People get on and off the next bus, but nobody who pays them any attention.

Only after the tennis court becomes free and Kennedy and Sarina start up a game does Kennedy notice a suspicious-looking guy walking his dog. A black baseball cap shades his face and he's wearing brown pants that ride low on his bum — plumber pants. She can see the outline of his belly button through his cheap white shirt. He walks around the park once, then comes and stations himself at the picnic table directly outside the tennis court fence. Kennedy watches him watching them and misses Sarina's next serve.

"Wake up over there," calls Sarina.

"Let's switch sides," says Kennedy, jogging toward the net.

"Don't look now," she says as they pass "but check out the guy sitting at the picnic table when we start playing again."

They switch sides and start playing again. After about fifteen minutes the guy gets up and leaves. They immediately stop playing and meet at the net.

"He's creepy enough," says Sarina.

"No kidding. Did you get a good picture of his face? Because next time you can bet he won't be wearing the ball cap or walking a dog. At least not the same dog."

"Brown hair, wide nose, close-set eyes and slightly overweight. How old would you say he is? Thirty?"

"I'd guess closer to forty."

Sarina shudders. "I'm not going to want to walk home by myself," she says, glancing over her shoulder.

"Let's go over to the skateboard park. Chase will be there. He'll protect you."

On the way to the skate park, they see Liam and his friend Sam rollerblading toward them along the sidewalk.

"Hey, Kennedy, hey, Sa-ri-na," calls out Liam with a salute.

Sarina waves but Kennedy doesn't bother, just steps onto the grass to avoid getting run over.

"Keep it cool," says Liam as he passes. "And watch out for creeptoids."

Sam is laughing, at nothing as far as she can tell. She never thought he was very smart.

Arriving home at three that afternoon, Kennedy finds a bleary-eyed Colin sitting up in his pullout bed, flicking through TV channels. The instant she sees him, shirtless and all, her nerves involuntarily stand at attention.

"Oh, hi," she says, trying to mute her excitement.

"Kennedy," says Colin, turning off the TV. "Oh god, I have to apologize for yesterday."

What part of yesterday? she wonders, noting the ripple of a six-pack as he turns to face her.

"I lost track of time and missed Elliot's taxi," he says, rolling his eyes. "Ended up exploring Victoria's club scene. You know, when in Rome ..." He shrugs, helplessly cute. "A couple of places weren't in the least interested in my age, so I drank far too much of one thing or another, I'm afraid. Just hope I didn't wake you when I came in?" He smiles his brilliant smile and pats the bed next to him. "Care to sit?"

Obediently Kennedy sits, and the next second he's leaning over and kissing the side of her head. She has to push back against him to keep from tipping over, can smell his minty breath. Thank god he brushed his teeth.

"No, you didn't wake me," she lies. "But you were missed."

"I know, it was terribly disloyal of me." Then he adds in a softer voice, "I like you, Kennedy."

She looks at him sideways, struggling to suppress an ear-splitting grin.

"Me too," she says and then realizes how moronic that sounded.

"It's a shame I'm not staying longer." He strokes her arm and Kennedy's eyes fall closed at the sensation. "Maybe you can come visit me in London?"

"Really?" she blurts, totally blowing her cool.

"Really," he laughs, inching closer. "So how did you like ..."

he mimes smoking a joint and then slips down farther on his pillow.

She can feel his warm breath on the exposed skin of her waist.

"Yeah, it was fun," she says.

He slides his hand down her arm again and, with his fingers, spreads her fingers apart. She holds her hand dumbly still where it's planted on the bed.

"I'm glad it was a good first experience," he says and catches her eye.

"Yeah." Unsure where this is headed, Kennedy removes her hand to brush the hair out of her eyes, then crosses her arms.

Colin takes a breath and sits up a little straighter.

"Sarina and I are trying to track down a stalker," she says, needing to change the subject.

"I thought a stalker tracks *you* down."

"I mean, there's this guy on MSN — that's our IM line — who calls himself Zak Smith and asks all these sick questions. He's obviously not our age. I mean, my age."

With his thumbnail, Colin starts cleaning his other nails.

She tells him about the plan to ferret him out and about the guy they saw at the park. "We're going to plant a meeting at the video store tonight to see if the same guy shows up." She knows she's talking too much and too fast but that's what happens when she's nervous. "Tomorrow we want to meet at a more secluded place because then we'd know for sure it was him. We're thinking of going down to Mount Doug beach and having a beach fire and stuff. Sarina and I were hoping you might want to come. It's pretty secluded, so we kind of want someone there as protection."

"Sure," he says with a thin laugh. "I understand I'm going whale watching with dear Mummy tomorrow, but we should be back by then."

"Great." Kennedy dares herself to kiss him on the cheek before darting up off the bed. "We're going to rent a movie tonight, if you're around." She remembers it's Harry Potter. He might think that's for kids.

"Maybe, if Mum doesn't keep me tied to her wrist."

Kennedy walks to her room with as much casual composure as she can muster. Once inside, she quietly locks the door behind her, then stands there feeling like a boiling kettle about to let loose its high-pitched screech. *Visit him in London? Well, no duh.* She starts jumping crazily from foot to foot around her room, shaking out her arms and legs and silently howling. This is way, way too much energy for her skin to contain.

"The adults and Colin are going out to the movies," Mom tells Kennedy that evening at dinner. "Sorry, it's rated R or we'd bring you along. But you and Sarina were going to watch a movie here tonight anyway, right? So how 'bout if I pay for that and you babysit Tory?"

Kennedy sighs. Go ahead, take Colin away and leave Tory behind.

"You're allowed a free kids' movie with your rental so Tory can watch upstairs and you and Sarina can have the downstairs. You won't have to do much, in other words."

"Okay," she agrees grudgingly. "But does Liam have to watch it with us?"

"Sam's in Vancouver tonight, so yes. Besides, what's so bad about that?"

Mom has no idea that she and Sarina might want to talk about things during movies, things that she doesn't care for her nosy little brother to overhear.

"We might go out afterward, but we shouldn't be too late," says Mom, handing her ten dollars. "Buy yourselves some treats."

Kennedy stands by the front door, watching the adults and Colin get in the car. Colin presses his wrists together at chest level to mime his imprisonment. Kennedy snickers and Dad glances around at Colin. With his invisibly tied hands, Colin awkwardly attempts to open the car door.

"Enjoy the movie," says Kennedy, smiling at his antics.

Colin manages to get in the car and shut the door behind him. He holds his cuffed wrists up so Kennedy can see them through the window. Kennedy stifles a laugh, then is startled as Judith's fast hands bat down her son's. His face hardens and he turns his head away from the window, away from Kennedy. She is both embarrassed and sad for him. Then the car is pulling away, Mom waving goodbye. Kennedy waves back. What a bitch Judith is. And she thought *her* mother was difficult.

Before the car's even out of sight, Tory's tugging on Kennedy's hand.

"Jump on the trampoline with me, Kendy. Now."

"We have to meet Sarina soon, Tory," she says, though they have a good twenty minutes to kill.

"But let's jump now," insists Tory, pulling on her.

Her sister's hand feels sticky and dirty both. "Only if you stop pulling on me," she threatens, and Tory instantly lets go. Maybe feeling so little warmth toward her sister is psychological evidence that Tory's only her half-sister. A half-blood. Kennedy follows Tory into the yard.

Bouncing in the middle of the trampoline, Kennedy dreams of being in the English countryside with Colin, on top of a double-decker bus, a Jane Austen tour bus. She's assuming there are Jane Austen tours, that is. Meanwhile, Tory springs around her singing "Baa Baa Black Sheep," changing the colour of the sheep with each new rendition. It's the song that never ends. Kennedy blocks Tory out by reliving yesterday's kiss. So amazing the feeling of his tongue against hers. Remembering Colin's firm hand on her breast, she spontaneously bounces high into the air. She lands hard and too close to Tory, who rebounds up into the air with a shriek. Tory lands on a clumsy angle and falls on her face, her head near the trampoline's thinly padded metal edge.

"Kendy, that's too hard," Tory whines.

"I'm sorry, Tor, I wasn't paying attention." Kennedy's heart flutters at the thought of Tory hitting her head, or worse, falling off. "You should be in the middle," she says, unloading her guilt. "I'll stay on the side."

"Okay," whimpers Tory, and she starts to stand but immediately sits back down. "My foot hurts." She starts to cry.

"Oh great," Kennedy says to the sky, then to Tory, "Let's see your foot."

The foot and ankle look perfectly normal, so Kennedy assumes, with a handful of hope thrown in, that Tory's just being dramatic to get attention.

"It'll be fine. Come on, it's time to meet Sarina," she says over Tory's crying. "We'll buy you an extra licorice at Mount Doug Market and then you can pick out your own movie at the video store." She lifts Tory off the trampoline. "Let me carry you to the stroller and I'll get Mom's ice pack to wrap around your foot." She tries hard to make these activities sound exciting. "The ice will make it all better," she adds in a soothing voice, but is suddenly unsure whether ice or heat is the appropriate measure.

"Mom's ice pack," Tory coughs through her tears. "I want Mom's ice pack."

Liam walks to the store with them. In the stroller Tory insists on holding her "hurt" foot straight out and up in the air. Wrapped in Mom's ice pack and covered with one of Dad's beige socks, Tory's tiny leg with the big beige ball at the end looks like a raw drumstick. Every few metres, Tory whines, "It still hurts, Kendy."

"It'll be fine, Tory, don't worry," she repeats.

To keep her mind off Tory's ankle, Kennedy confides in Liam about her and Sarina's plan to trap Zak the pervert and about the guy they saw at Majestic, "just before you and Sam showed up."

"Zak" and "perver" is what Tory picks out of the conversation and she proceeds to chant it under her breath. "Zak Perver, Zak Perver," as if it's somebody name.

Liam seems utterly thrilled by the idea. "Project: trapping the perv diggity," says Liam. "Hella thinking for a couple of girl-things. Zak the man could be after us boys too, you know. Boy toys. Sexy young things like me." Walking with his arms glued to his sides, Liam swings his hips and puckers his lips. "It's my gay parade walk," he says, waving an imaginary little flag. "He could be stalking me as we speak."

A car comes up the street and he shades his eyes to peer in its passing window.

"Cut it out, Liam," says Kennedy. "You're embarrassing me."

"Our man Zak probably drives a white van. A white van with curtains in the back." He raises his pale eyebrows. "Lime green curtains."

Flower bouquets line the outside walls of Mount Doug Market. Kennedy spies a dozen red velvet roses. After Judith and Colin are gone, she's definitely going to buy some on Dad's behalf. She'll tell Dad he needs to up the romance quota. Insist that Mom needs that sort of thing in her life right now. She sees Sarina through the store window and wheels Tory and her chicken leg inside.

"No sign of him yet," Sarina whispers to Kennedy before squatting down to give Tory a hello and a hug.

"Whatever happened to your little foot?" Sarina coos.

"Kendy made me fall."

"Oh?" She looks to Kennedy.

"We were on the tramp," says Kennedy. "It was an accident. She's fine."

"It hurts," pouts Tory.

"Here, come pick out a licorice, Tory," says Kennedy.

"You said I could have two."

They pay for an assortment of licorice whips and a large bag of chips, then head across the street to Video Stop. Kennedy gives Tory a licorice to keep her quiet. A black mutt is tied to a pipe in front of the store. Tory wants to pet it.

"You don't pet strange dogs," says Kennedy.

"Doesn't that look like *his* dog?" Sarina says, stopping.

Kennedy studies the dog again. "There's a lot of black dogs around."

"I'll see if he's inside," offers Liam.

"I want to pet the dog," whines Tory.

"No, you can't," Kennedy says, trying to address both siblings at once. "Liam, wait. You don't even know what he looks like. And god, don't do anything jerky if we see him. It doesn't necessarily mean anything yet."

"I'm cool," says Liam, narrowing his eyes and running a slow hand through his hair. "Hella cool."

Kennedy sighs.

"Hi doggy," says Tory, reaching out her licorice as they pass by. The dog wags his tail happily, straining his leash in order to sniff the red candy.

Sarina leads the way into the store, and standing right there at the counter, not two metres away, is the guy from the park, still dressed in his baseball cap, thin white shirt and saggy brown pants. He glances over at them, smiles a fleeting smile. Of recognition? wonders Kennedy. Sarina instinctively backs up right into the stroller and Tory's foot. Tory lets go a blood curdling scream. The whole store is looking at them now as Kennedy takes Sarina by the arm, hushes a screeching Tory and, steering the stroller with one hand, leads them all to the back of the store.

"Is that him?" asks Liam, grinning like a maniac.

Sarina nods, wide-eyed.

"Quiet," hisses Kennedy to both Liam and her crying sister.

"I'm so sorry," says Sarina, bending down to wipe Tory's face. Tory's crying settles into a mournful whimper.

With several rows of videos between them, they all watch Creepy Guy take his movie and leave. Through the window they see him untie his dog, who's yelping and jumping madly at his return. Before walking away, Creepy Guy glances up at the window. Kennedy and Sarina quickly look away, but Liam smiles and waves.

"What are you doing?" Kennedy smacks Liam's arm.

"I'm just being friendly."

"This is not a joke, Liam."

"Oh my god," says Sarina. "It's got to be him."

"Kendy, my foot hurts," whines Tory.

"It'll feel better soon, I promise," she says, praying it's true.

Liam hooks his thumb under the collar of his T-shirt and stretches it up to his mouth. "Closing in on Zak Smith, Z. S., the perv-diggity," he whispers into his collar as if into a lapel microphone. "And perv-diggity's dog, Chuck."

"Well, that's two out of two," says Kennedy. "If he shows up at the beach, then how can there be any doubt?"

"Kendy, it hurts," Tory says again, her whine rising to an impossibly irritating pitch.

"Why don't you," Kennedy says calmly, squatting down beside Tory and kissing her tear-stained cheeks, "go pick out a movie from the centre aisle there?"

"Okay," she whimpers and starts out of the stroller. One step on the drumstick foot and she falls to her knees. "I can't walk." She starts to cry again.

Sarina picks Tory up and puts her back in the stroller. "Poor sweetie. I'll take you over. Do you think maybe it's sprained, Kennedy?"

Kennedy shakes her head, then squats down in front of her sister. "Tory, we'll get your foot its own special pillow when we get home and you can watch your movie. Here, let's take your ice sock off now," she says, remembering something about a ten-minute rule for ice. She sees that Tory's first licorice is gone and offers the second one. Tory quiets down for the time being and they get their movies and leave.

Outside, Kennedy does a quick scan of the cars and vans in the parking lot, just in case Creepy Guy is hanging around waiting to follow them home or something. She does a double take when she sees Elliot getting out of his taxi. He's dressed in more fashionable clothes — baggy army-green shorts and black collared T-shirt — and he's holding a movie in one hand. Must be returning it, she figures, though she doesn't recall ever seeing him around here before.

"Hey, there's Elliot," says Sarina, waving him over.

"Hi," he says, looking as serious as ever. "Getting a movie?" He directs the question to Kennedy.

"Harry," says Liam in his best English accent, "Harry Potter." He holds up the video.

"This is my brother Liam and my sister Tory," says Kennedy.

"Hey," he says to Liam, and reaches out to shake his hand.

So adult, thinks Kennedy, watching an unsure Liam return the shake. Elliot kneels down to Tory's level.

"Kendy and Sarina hurt my foot," pouts Tory, chewing on her red licorice whip.

"I'm sorry to hear that," Elliot says, glancing up at the girls.

"Accident," says Sarina, "really and truly."

He looks at Tory's hurt ankle, then at the other ankle.

"You live nearby?" asks Kennedy. "I've never seen you around here."

"Not far," he answers.

"Took out my handiwork, I see," says Sarina, pointing to his hair.

He smiles slightly and again looks at Kennedy.

"Your sister's ankle is really swollen."

"It is?" She kneels beside him to look for herself. It's true. Tory's ankle is twice the size of the other and the underside is black and blue.

"Oh my god," says Kennedy, her gut knotting with guilt.

"I want Mommy," says Tory, mournfully.

"It's okay, Tory, we'll take care of it." Kennedy lifts her sister out of her seat and into her arms. "I'm so sorry. I had no idea it was this hurt." Elliot must think she's an irresponsible idiot. Kennedy looks at Sarina. "What am I supposed to do?" she mouths, panicky.

"I could drive you to the clinic. It's open until nine." Elliot points to his car.

"I guess we should," says Kennedy, unsure.

"Do I have to come?" says Liam.

"I could drive Liam home first," says Elliot.

"We better take her," says Sarina.

Kennedy asks Elliot if he really doesn't mind doing this.

"No problem," he says with a smile. A real smile this time.

His whole face changes when he smiles, Kennedy notes once again.

"Can I ride in the front?" asks Liam.

"Sure." Elliot opens the back door of the cab for Kennedy and holds it until she and Tory are safely inside. He folds up the stroller and puts it in the trunk.

"We can walk home from the clinic," Kennedy says when Elliot gets in the car. "So you don't have to wait."

"I'm not doing anything." He starts up the car.

"Oh, you forgot to take back your movie," remembers Sarina.

Elliot hesitates. "It's not due till tomorrow anyway."

"This isn't from Video Stop, it's from Rogers," says Liam, picking up the movie on the seat beside him.

"Oh," says Elliot with a nervous laugh. "My mom must have told me the wrong place. Good thing I didn't take it inside."

Kennedy's not sure she believes him. But why would he be lying?

The nurse behind the front desk gives them a fresh ice pack and three orange-flavoured painkillers for Tory. Sarina offers to read Tory one of the oversized kids' books in the magazine rack.

"Really, you don't have to wait," Kennedy tells Elliot.

"I know." He sits down directly across from her.

It's been too weird a night, and a guilt-ridden Kennedy just wants to escape into the *People* magazine on the coffee table between them. Angelina Jolie is on the cover with her multiracial family.

"Have you had any more trouble from that Zak character?" asks Elliot.

"As a matter of fact —" Kennedy starts, but Sarina jumps in.

"We planted two meetings online and this guy showed up at both places."

Elliot nods gravely.

"Yeah," continues Kennedy. "He was watching us play tennis at the park and then he smiled at us at the video store tonight. He was there just before you showed up."

"I was afraid of that," says Elliot, and for a few seconds Kennedy finds herself lost in the warm brown of his eyes. No, they're more amber than brown.

"We're going to plant a meeting at a secluded beach," says Sarina. "So if he shows then, we'll know for sure."

"You're not going alone?" he says in that condescending tone of his, and Kennedy feels herself bristle.

"No, Colin's coming with us."

"No worries with Colin around." His voice drips sarcasm. "Did he make his way home last night?"

"He did." She doesn't bother with details.

The nurse calls "Victoria Baines" and Kennedy, relieved to get away from Mr. Know-it-all, gets up and wheels Tory down the hall.

"You her mother?" asks the doctor, squinting at her over his glasses.

"Her sister."

"Oh, yes."

He feels around the swollen ankle until Tory screams and lunges for Kennedy, clasping her neck in a death grip.

"The growth plate, I'd say. Common occurrence at this age." He speaks in curt, choppy sentences as if running short of breath. "Breaks in that area don't show up on X-ray. The bone's not fully calcified yet. Might as well head to emergency. Get a cast on her."

"It's broken?"

"The ankle's fractured, yes. I'll give you the forms. You'll need a parent's signature —"

"I don't know if I can get in touch with them. They're at the movies."

"Well, I'll sign it and yours will have to suffice in this case."

"Okay."

"Fibreglass is best for this age. Three weeks is all she'll need. And you, little miss," he says to Tory, "will be able to choose the colour of your cast. Do you have a favourite?"

Tory won't answer him after he hurt her like that.

"Purple, I think," offers Kennedy as the reality begins to sink in: she broke her little sister's ankle.

PAIN #20: BREAKING THINGS

Kennedy mentally tallies the things she's broken in recent months: her MP3 when it went through the wash, the strap on her favourite purse when it caught on the doorknob, her new sunglasses when she sat on them in the car, and now her sister's anklebone. Half-sister or not, Kennedy feels wretched.

Back in the waiting room, avoiding Elliot's critical eye, she informs Sarina and Elliot of the situation.

"That's terrible," says Sarina, her hand covering her mouth.

Tory smiles at Sarina's reaction. Kennedy's relieved to
see her smiling. The painkillers must be kicking in.

"Well, let's go get her a cast, then," says Elliot.

"Are you sure?" asks Kennedy, feeling he's done too
much already.

"I'm sure." He walks over to the exit door and holds it
open for them.

PAIN #21: FEELING INDEBTED TO PEOPLE

She never knew if and when she'd be able to pay back
other people's kindnesses. Mom told Kennedy that accept-
ing people's gifts and favours is payback in itself, but that
never really washed with her.

It's ten o'clock by the time they pull into Kennedy's driveway. From the knee down, Tory's leg is wrapped in a neon-
yellow, glow-in-the-dark walking cast. The technician at the
hospital said it would be a couple of days before Tory
could comfortably put weight on her foot, and Sarina
offers to carry her upstairs.

"That was so nice of you, Elliot," says Sarina, and
Kennedy has to agree.

Feeling as if she owes Elliot big-time now, Kennedy asks
if he wants a drink or something. "Or you could stay and
watch the movie with us?"

"No, thanks," he says. "I should probably go."

"Okay." She's glad. She's tired — exhausted, really, and
just wants to flake out with Sarina and the movie. Or if
Colin makes it home, watch it leaning on his shoulder,
his strong arm around her waist.

"Is Colin here?" he asks.

"He's out with my parents and his mom. They should be back any minute," she says, afraid that Elliot might change his mind and stay.

"Well, I should go. Good night," he says and bows his head slightly before catching himself and lifting his hand instead.

"Thanks again for everything," she says and closes the door.

In the living room, Liam's watching the tail end of the movie, an empty bag of chips on the floor. Tory is hopping across the floor on one foot and turning off all the lights.

"My cast glows in the dark," she says happily.

"Willow called," says Liam. "Wants you and Sarina to call her ASAP. Big-C crisis." He says this in a flat monotone.

"What now?" says Kennedy, trudging toward the phone.

16

"Willow's upset." Amber has answered the phone at Willow's.

"What's happened?" asks Kennedy.

"Graham dumped her. Can we come over?"

"Sure, I guess."

Although Willow and Kennedy have never been all that close, Kennedy has trouble saying no to people. She has a reputation among their group of being a good listener and saying the right things when someone's upset. Kennedy has no idea if she's truly helpful, but she does try to listen. Tonight, though, she's hardly up for it.

Kennedy sets up Tory in the easy chair with a "special pillow" for her foot, a blanket, a snack plate and drink, then puts on her Rugrats movie. It's way past her bedtime, but Tory's refused to go to bed before she can show Mom, Dad and Judith her cast and Kennedy is not about to argue. She and Sarina are starting downstairs to finally watch their movie when Tory stops them with two words. "It itches."

"What itches?"

"My ankle."

Kennedy looks at Tory's leg encased from knee to toes in neon cement.

"Well, you can't scratch it, so don't think about it. Watch your movie. It'll go away."

"No, it's not, Kendy," Tory whines.

Kennedy's going to scream. She looks wide-eyed at Sarina for help.

"My dad broke his arm once playing hockey, and he used to slide a chopstick down his cast when it itched," says Sarina.

"Mommy has chopsticks," says Tory. "It's itching."

Not a single one of Mom's rainbow assortment of chopsticks is long enough to reach "the spot" on Tory's ankle.

"That's not the spot," she complains and points lower on her impenetrable blazing yellow leg. "Ow, it's itching!" She's close to tears now.

Ten minutes and several sticklike items later, Kennedy finds a Slurpee spoon-straw that reaches the itch. As Kennedy jimmies the straw up and down, Tory sighs with contentment. "Good and now start my movie over, please. I missed the song at the beginning."

"Oh my god," moans Kennedy.

"I'll do it," says Sarina.

"Finally," says Kennedy, dropping onto the couch, aka Colin's bed. "Tory should fall asleep in about thirty seconds."

She digs around for the remote.

"So this is where the man sleeps?" says Sarina, stroking the arm of the couch.

"Stop it," smiles Kennedy. Before she even finds the remote, the doorbell rings.

"Willow and Amber," says Sarina. "I'll get it."

Kennedy wishes they weren't coming over. She just wants to watch the movie, or better yet, crawl into bed with her book. She's getting to such a sweet part because Elizabeth is beginning to admire and fall in love with Mr. Darcy. Elizabeth takes a trip to the country with her aunt and uncle and they pass very near the palatial Pemberley manor, which is Mr. Darcy's home. Learning that the family is away in London, Elizabeth's aunt insists they take a tour. Mr. Darcy unexpectedly arrives, much to Elizabeth's embarrassment, but he appears supremely happy about the coincidence. Oh yes, thinks Kennedy longingly, I just want to be transported to Pemberley manor.

Wearing pink shorts that barely cover her bum and a top that is more bra than shirt, Willow sulks into the rec room and plunks down on the couch. She must have been trying to torture Graham with that outfit, thinks Kennedy. Willow crosses her arms and legs with a little huff and her breasts nearly pop out of her so-called top. Kennedy can hear Amber whispering to Sarina in the hall.

"Hi, Willow," says Kennedy, finally seeing the remote beside Tory's dress-up box. "I'm so sorry about you and Graham."

Willow is pouting and looking in the direction of the window.

"You broke your sister's leg?" asks Amber, coming through the door.

"It's a fractured ankle," says Kennedy, giving Sarina a look. "And it was an accident."

"My parents would kill me if I broke my brother's leg." Amber plops down on the couch.

"Well, mine aren't going to be too thrilled," says Kennedy.

Amber shakes her head at Willow, who's now staring glumly at the blank TV. "Graham is such a pig. Tell her, you guys, nobody likes him, do they?"

"If he doesn't like you," confirms Sarina, "we don't like him."

Willow chews her lips and examines her peeling red nail polish.

"You can do better, Willow," says Kennedy. "A lot better."

"He's a great kisser," says Willow softly. "And his nose fits perfectly in my ear." She pets her right ear and Kennedy and Sarina exchange glances.

"It was one of their little things," explains Amber.

"Watching a movie will help you forget about him," says Kennedy, flicking on the TV. It's getting late and if they don't start it now, it won't happen. She presses *play*.

"I saw this movie with Graham," Willow says in a small voice.

Kennedy turns the volume way down.

Changing topics, Sarina tells them about the stalker guy and their beach plans for tomorrow night. "We're bringing Colin for protection."

"Who's Colin?" asks Amber.

"A total hunk from England who sleeps on this very couch.

Eighteen and sexy. Harry Potter accent. It's too great. He calls cops 'bobbies'."

"When's he coming back?" asks Willow.

"No idea." Kennedy inches up the volume.

They watch the movie in peace for a whole ten minutes before there's the rumble of a car pulling into the drive. Colin, thinks Kennedy, sitting up and running a hand over her hair.

"Your folks?" says Sarina.

"Must be."

"And Colin," Sarina says to Willow. "Wait till you see him. He'll make you forget all about Graham."

Willow drags the elastic from her thick chocolate-brown hair, bends over to flip her hair forward, then comes up, tossing it back to fan out over her shoulders. With her small, flat-faced features, Willow's always been considered more cute than pretty, a tough kind of cute. Kennedy stares at her, amazed at the sudden transformation from hurt, pouty girl into confident sex kitten. She hopes Willow hasn't forgotten about Graham and his nose entirely.

Kennedy suddenly remembers Tory's broken ankle and gets up off the couch. "I better go tell Mom about Tory."

"Do you have any popcorn?" asks Amber.

"I can make some," offers Kennedy, and immediately wishes she hadn't.

"That would be great." Amber's whole face lights up.

Kennedy goes out, closing the door behind her, and runs smack into Colin.

"Oh, hi. How was your evening?" she says, her heart picking up speed.

"Movie was depressing, tapas bar after was delicious, but boring without you there," he says, then takes her hand and kisses her knuckles.

She wants to throw her arms around him but plays it cool.

"And yours?" he asks.

"You don't want to know," she sighs, then starts past him but he playfully blocks her way. "I have to catch Mom before she sees Tory's cast." He doesn't budge.

"Colin," she scolds, smiling. "Really, Tory broke her ankle and I have to explain how it happened."

"Can't you get by?" he teases, not seeming to have heard.

She looks him in the eye, takes a breath and dares to shove him hard on the shoulder. He gives way easily and she trips clumsily past. He laughs and she swats at him and misses, making him laugh more.

"I'll get you for that," she says, hurrying up the stairs.

"I'll look forward to it," he says with a wink, and Kennedy's knees go soft.

"My friends and I are watching a movie," she says over the banister. "Sorry, but we're using your bed."

"Sounds fine to me."

Tory is asleep in her chair, her cast hidden by the blanket Kennedy covered her with. Mom and Judith are standing over her, cooing about the way Tory's sleeping on folded hands. Kennedy assumes Dad's already hiding in the bedroom, reading.

"Like a little angel," says Judith in a slow, plodding voice.

She sounds tipsy, if not drunk.

"Hi," says Kennedy, trying to think of a way to fudge the truth concerning her sister's ankle. Why bother? Tory will fill Mom in on every detail soon enough.

"Kennedy," says Judith, her eyelids drooping as she steadies herself on the back of Tory's chair. "Such a pretty girl you are. Tall too. You look older than sixteen."

"I'm fifteen," she corrects.

Definitely drunk, thinks Kennedy, and she wonders why a drunk adult looks so much more pathetic than a drunk teenager. Although it's a shame that Mom looks so perfectly sober.

Kennedy explains "the accident" on the trampoline, then says how they ran into Elliot, who drove them to the clinic, and how the doctor said this sort of break was "extremely" common in this age group. "Then we had to go all the way to the hospital." When she lifts up the blanket and reveals the leg, Judith stares at Kennedy in horror, then looks as if she's going to cry. Mom is frowning, a tight-lipped frown.

"It's been such a long night," continues Kennedy. "We just got home a half hour ago. I'm exhausted," she adds, trying to garner some sympathy for all *she's* had to endure.

Mom looks at Tory and shakes her head. "Kennedy," is all she says.

Right, all my fault, thinks Kennedy defensively, yet she has to admit it's true. This one *is* all her fault.

She gives Mom the cast-care pamphlet from the hospital, apologizes one more time and hurries back downstairs. Then she remembers she promised Amber she'd make popcorn. Shit.

By the time the popcorn's popped, the butter's melted and she's answered Mom's accusing questions, nobody except Amber is in the rec room watching the movie.

"Oh thanks, Kennedy," says Amber, reaching for the bowl. "Willow and Sarina are outside with that Bobby guy," she explains, taking up a handful of popcorn, her eyes fixed on the TV.

"Oh?"

Kennedy looks from the movie and inviting couch to the rec room door.

"I'll be right back," she says. She goes into her bedroom to look out the window.

Colin, Willow and Sarina are standing around the ping-pong table, laughing. Colin's smoking and doing the talking, clearly charming them with his wit. Willow's crossed arms totally exaggerate her cleavage and Colin can't seem to keep his eyes off her. Kennedy slides open the window.

PAIN #22: JEALOUSY

It makes her teeth ache.

"Hey, guys, come watch the movie," she calls, trying unsuccessfully to pry Colin's eyes away from Willow's boobs. "There's popcorn."

"In a minute," says Willow, tossing both her words and her hair over her shoulder.

Kennedy shuts the window. Only Sarina starts toward the door. No, thinks Kennedy in a panic, we can't leave a freshly dumped Willow alone with Colin.

"Come watch with me, Kennedy," Amber is calling. "This is a freaky part."

Kennedy leaves her room, hesitates by the door to the carport, then settles beside Amber on the couch.

Sarina comes and joins them.

"Aren't Willow and Colin coming?" asks Kennedy.

"I thought so." Sarina reaches past her for some popcorn, then stops. "You're not jealous, are you?" she whispers.

"Well, Willow seems to have gotten over Graham pretty quick," Kennedy whispers back.

"Ssh," says Amber. "Just watch."

Kennedy tries to focus on the movie, but after several minutes and still no sign of Colin and Willow, she gets up and heads for the carport. It's not Willow's fault, she reasons. She has no idea that Colin is already spoken for. Why didn't Kennedy mention it earlier?

"Well, he's an idiot for breaking up with you," she hears Colin say as she opens the door.

Willow, looking forlorn and waiflike, smiles up at him. "He was a bore, really."

Was that a hint of an English accent?

"Hey," says Kennedy, as casually as possible.

Colin's hand is resting on the ping-pong table behind Willow, who's standing so close to him it looks as if that hand is touching her bum. When he sees Kennedy, he lifts his hidden hand and rakes his fingers through his hair.

Kennedy forces herself to walk up to Colin and stroke his arm. Colin looks surprised but pleased. Then his hand is suddenly around her waist as if claiming her right back. Willow is staring at Kennedy, open-mouthed. Kennedy gives her an apologetic smile. She feels better now, yet she doesn't want Colin to think she's anything like Willow. Promiscuous, that is. Though she doesn't want him to think her a prude, either. Because she isn't. She's cautious, is all, and inexperienced.

"I thought you were still with Jordan," says Willow, and Kennedy's thoughts start racing.

"Well," she says, picturing Willow telling Amber, who'll mention it to Chase, and how awful it would be for Jordan to hear it from someone else first. "Colin and I are just friends." She gives Colin's shoulder a friendly shove and catches his eye.

"Buddies," says Colin with a shove back, and Kennedy wonders what he must think of her. She's never mentioned Jordan before.

"Oh," says Willow, smiling again.

"Jordan's on vacation right now, up-island," says Kennedy to Colin. "Too bad you won't meet him."

"Too bad," says Colin.

"Maybe we should go in," she suggests.

Willow shrugs and moves toward the door in her skimpy shorts.

"Sure," agrees Colin, his hand brushing across Kennedy's bum as she starts to follow Willow.

She gives him a look over her shoulder and his grinning face has an animal hunger about it. Turning back around, she imagines Colin mutating onto all fours behind her, like the kids did in her old Animorph books. He'd be what? she muses. A black panther, maybe.

Inside, Amber sits in the middle of the couch, clutching a pillow to her chest, intent on the movie. Sarina is on her left, holding the popcorn bowl and eating one kernel at a time.

"You take the couch, Willow," Kennedy says, hoping to keep her away from Colin. "I'll sit on the floor."

"Can we turn off the lights?" Colin asks, settling into the armchair.

"Sure." Kennedy flips off the lamp.

"I like this part," says Sarina, "when the teams come in? It's so cool."

Kennedy starts to find a spot on the floor but Colin grabs her by a belt loop and pulls her onto the narrow arm of his chair. She's glad it's dark and that Willow, from where she's sitting, can't see Colin's arm around Kennedy's hip, fingering the edge of her shorts. In the safe presence of her friends, Colin's physical attentions are welcome and thrilling. Her perch on the chair arm is truly uncomfortable but she doesn't dare move and halt the heavenly sensation of his hand on her thigh. After a little while, his index finger slips up her shorts and runs under the elastic of her underwear. Her head flushes with heat and her crotch tingles. She doesn't dare look at him in case he thinks she's liking it too much. She stares hard at the movie but registers little else but Colin's hand. But she does hear the creak of the stairs. She checks the clock on the VCR. It's nearly eleven-thirty, curfew time. Must be Dad.

"My dad's coming," she whispers to Colin, slipping off the chair arm to sit on the floor.

The door opens and the light from the hall slices into the dark.

"Kennedy," comes her dad's shy voice.

"Hi, Dad," she says.

"I expect your friends are leaving at eleven-thirty?"

"They will, don't worry."

He does a double take. To locate Colin amongst the girls?

"Kennedy, can I talk to you for a minute?"

Kennedy gets up and goes out in the hall, closing the door behind her.

"I'm off tomorrow, sweetheart. Two nights up in Prince George."

"Oh?" She didn't know, or at least didn't remember.

"So, take care of yourself." He kisses her on the forehead. "Must have been quite a night for you, what with Tory breaking her ankle. You did the right thing. Just sorry we weren't here to help."

"Me too. It was not what I call fun," she says, grateful to him for seeing her side of it.

"So," he hesitates, "Judith and Colin are here for another four nights."

"Yeah." She knows what he's trying to say. "It's okay, we'll be fine." He should be more worried about Mom than me, thinks Kennedy, flashing on that David guy from the café.

He turns to go. "Don't stay up too late."

"I won't," she says, then quickly hugs him. "Have a good trip."

He starts up the stairs and Kennedy opens the door to the rec room.

"Turn on the light in there, please," Dad calls over the banister, trying to sound authoritative.

"Right, Dad." She smiles to herself.

"You guys have to go now, sorry." She turns on the lamp to see Willow kneeling by Colin's chair, whispering in his ear.

"But it's not over," complains Amber.

"You can take it home, Amber. Don't forget it's due by four tomorrow, though."

Move, Willow, thinks Kennedy. Move away from him.

"Thanks, Kennedy, I will," says Amber.

Colin laughs at whatever it is that Willow said and Willow smiles and stands up.

"I'll call my mom." Sarina takes out her cell phone. "She can probably give you guys a ride," she says to Willow and Amber.

"Great," Amber answers for them both.

"Nice to meet you, Colin," Willow says in her best twinkie voice.

"You too, Willow." He kisses her hand the way he did Kennedy's earlier, and Willow twitters happily, turns on her heel and swishes away.

17

Kennedy takes the empty popcorn bowl up to the kitchen. The house is quiet, all the lights turned out. As she passes Liam's room, she hears him grumbling in his sleep. "No ... it's not ... no ... I'm ... all along." God, he doesn't even shut up in his sleep. There's no sliver of a reading light under her parents' door and she hears someone snoring: a loud, sloppy snore. Dad? No, she thinks, it's coming from Judith's room.

She and Colin are the only ones awake, muses Kennedy on her way back downstairs. It's kind of like they're alone in the house. As she opens the door to the rec room, her heart is thudding in her ears. Colin's bed is pulled out but he's not in it. Must be outside having a smoke. She slips into the bathroom to get ready for bed. After washing her face, brushing her teeth and spraying her hair with anti-frizz product, she decides to leave her contacts in and slips the contact case into her pocket. She'll remove them in her bedroom. Imagine sleeping the night in Colin's arms. Not having sex, just sleeping together, snuggled warm and close, their breathing synchronized, dreaming their separate dreams. On the way to her room, she smells smoke through the opened window and deliberately leaves her bedroom door unlocked.

After she changes into her La Senza pyjamas, Kennedy picks up *Pride and Prejudice* and climbs into bed. Keeping one ear open for Colin, she reads up to where Elizabeth learns, via letter, that her youngest sister Lydia has eloped — with Mr. Wickham! Lydia is sixteen. And Wickham, Elizabeth can guess, has no plans of actually marrying Lydia, but only taking advantage and moving on. While the Bennet household bemoans Lydia's scandalous circumstance, Elizabeth bemoans knowing the possibility of Mr. Darcy ever renewing his marriage proposal to her is now doomed — not to mention her sisters' prospects of securing a fortunate marriage. Elizabeth blames herself for not having revealed Wickham's devious nature when she had the chance.

Kennedy hears Colin come inside from the carport, the door shutting and the lock being clicked across. She lowers the book to her lap and listens. She hears faint sounds of water running in the bathroom, the toilet flushing. She listens for the creaking sounds of his climbing into bed, but the next sound is a light knock on her door.

"Kennedy?"

Definitely not Dad this time, she thinks, taking a calming breath. She decides against putting on her robe, gets up and goes to the door. She opens it, but only partway.

"Yes?"

"I just want to say goodnight."

"Oh. Goodnight, Colin." She has to work to keep her voice from shaking.

"Just one kiss?" he asks in a tone so velvety soft, her eyelids suddenly feel heavy.

She opens the door a little wider and his hands are instantly holding the sides of her face, his mouth inhaling hers. His mint-flavoured tongue pushes into her mouth, runs along the front, then back of her teeth. Mirroring his tongue-work the best she can, Kennedy kisses him back. He steps closer and their bodies press together, his hands moving from her face to her back. He's strong, she thinks, aware of the thinness of the material between him and her bare chest. It's a totally awesome moment, yet her brain won't stop questioning if it's right. If she can trust him. She pulls softly away and he follows her lead, his hands sliding from her back to either side of her ribs just under her arms. The thumb of his left hand nudges the outside curve of her breast.

"Well, goodnight," she says again, and his hands slowly slip away. She steps behind the door again, using it like some kind of shield.

"Tomorrow, then," he sighs, his dark blue eyes flickering down to her chest. "You're awfully pretty, you know," he adds, not moving from the doorway.

Kennedy feels herself blush. She slowly starts shutting the door, forcing him to retreat. The door clicks into place and this time she locks it. Back in bed, she grabs her book to press it down over her thumping heart. She hears the creak of the couch bed as the TV comes on. Should she have gone further? He's only here for a few more days. Does he think she's a prude? What will it take for him not to forget her? She's not ready for sex, but there's other things they could do.

If only she were bold enough to tell him up front that

she doesn't want to have sex but would like to sleep next to him, maybe fool around a bit. But god, what if Dad came down? Nightmare. Mom, on the other hand, would probably go fish some condoms out of her purse.

She remembers her contacts and pops them out and into their cleaning case. She forces her attention back to her book, to the Bennet household, which is becoming the talk of the town, the family's reputation ruined right along with Lydia's virtue. Mr. Bennet and Elizabeth's uncle have gone off to London to search for Lydia and somehow to force Wickham to marry her and salvage the situation.

It's a long time before Kennedy's body and mind calm down enough to let her fall asleep.

Too early the next morning the phone wakes her up. It's Sarina.

"Kennedy, sorry to call so early. Did I wake you?"

"Uh-huh."

"Oh, sorry. But I wanted to tell you that I can't do the beach thing tonight because I'm going to Pender Island for the day with my parents. Both of them. They want to have the big talk, I guess."

"That's good," mumbles Kennedy, eyes still shut. "I'm so glad."

"Maybe if I cry enough, they'll think twice. Or if I make sure we have such a great time together, then maybe they won't want to mess things up. Anyway, you're asleep so I'll let you go. But let's plan the beach thing for tomorrow instead. All right?"

"All right."

"Send it over MSN. Bye and wish me luck."

"Luck."

Kennedy rolls over and goes back to sleep.

By the time Kennedy's out of bed, it's just before noon and Colin is gone. He doesn't appear to be outside or upstairs, and neither does Judith. Mom is sitting at the kitchen table studying her script and Liam is making a sandwich and slicing onions. He looks up at Kennedy and grins maniacally, showing his teeth. Tears are streaming from his eyes. She forgets to laugh. Remembering that Dad left this morning, Kennedy takes a long look at her mother. Not stoned yet, she decides, though dirty breakfast dishes are piled by the sink.

"Where's Judith?" she asks.

"She took Colin whale watching," says Mom. "Those poor whales. Day in, day out, it's like they're being stalked."

Definitely not stoned if she's ranting about whales. Kennedy's heard her mother's whale speech before and heads for the cereal cupboard.

"All those motors roaring under the water. It's making them crazy, you know. The babies aren't surviving."

"There's been a cougar sighting," says Liam, feeding Mom's fire. "Yesterday. Over on Blenkinsop Road." He sniffs back onion tears for dramatic effect. "They're probably going to kill it."

"I heard," says Mom. "And you know, the authorities are thinking of doing a cull. A cull!" She shakes her shorn head.

"Humans are the dangerous ones. We have to stop the urban sprawl. Can you even begin to imagine a planet without wildlife?"

PAIN #23: PASSIONATE INACTION

Kennedy can't bear listening to Mom go on about something that she's not willing to actually do anything about. It makes Kennedy feel helpless and defeated. If Mom can't help change the problems of the world, what can *she* possibly do?

Tory comes hopping around the corner on her good leg.

"Look at me, I'm a one-legged rabbit."

She's wearing white bunny ears with pink satin centres and her two hands are curled into paws at her chest. The ears are part of a costume from Kennedy's one and only ballet concert and a memento Kennedy would have saved for posterity if only Tory were a boy. It's lunchtime, Kennedy notes, and Tory's still in pyjamas. It's starting. Mom will be toking up anytime now.

"How's the ankle feel?" asks a sincerely sorry Kennedy.

"You broke it!" Tory answers, hopping past.

"It was an accident," says Mom. "It'll be good as new in a few weeks."

"But I can't go to the pool or the water park," chimes Tory. "Or take a bath."

"No bath," says Liam. "You'll be one gamey rabbit."

"No. Mommy will wash me in the sink."

"One odorous hare. One raunchy rodent. One putrid pet."

"I won't," yells Tory.

"The B.O. bunny," continues Liam, and Tory hops over and kicks him with her cast.

"Ow! That hurts."

"Tory and Liam, that's enough," says Mom.

Kennedy can't handle the noise and takes her cereal downstairs. Sarina's gone. Colin's gone. What should she do today?

She sees the box of pictures she's been saving for a collage — one of her summer projects along with rereading *Pride and Prejudice* and getting a job. She wants to cover one entire side of her bedroom door with old pictures of friends and mix in cutouts from magazines: punchy words, interesting expressions, funky pictures of body parts, animals, birds, whatever. And then she's going to detail it with these tiny mirror squares that came off a disco ball Liam bought at a yard sale, and he and Sam promptly destroyed. She mentally adds another project to her list — figure out the *Moulin Rouge* love song medley on the keyboard, the duet between Ewan McGregor and Nicole Kidman. She loves how part of one love song leads into another. Shouldn't be too hard to pick out.

Finishing her cereal, she puts on her *Moulin Rouge* CD, locates the glue and gets to work. She sings as she cuts up magazines, performing both parts, tenor and soprano. "Just one night, give me just one night. There's no way, 'cause you can't pay."

She can sing way better than Kidman, she tells herself. The woman has zero power behind her voice. As Kennedy's voice warms, she feels her chest and diaphragm soften. Soon she gets that nice hollowed-out feeling, as if her torso were a wind instrument playing itself. "In the name of love, one night in the name of love," she belts into the room, pushing out the walls. "You crazy fool, I won't give in to you."

Singing is such a release, muses Kennedy. It's the one time she feels that she can let go, express herself without holding back. Without double-thinking everything. Often it feels as if it's someone else's voice entirely, not hers, doing the singing.

She starts at the base of the door where she pastes her oldest pictures, the ones from Fredericton, when she was in grade four and had short hair and those goofy blue-rimmed glasses. There's her best friends, Martha and Kathleen. And there's her first so-called boyfriend, Charlie Breau, and his rat tail. She remembers the time he kissed her, close-mouthed, behind the jungle gym, once and only once before they "broke up."

Kennedy eyes her camera on the bookshelf and tells herself she must take a picture of Colin. Who knows how long until they'll see each other again? Maybe she'll get him to pose without his shirt on.

The song ends and she uses the remote to play it again, emptying herself into each note.

Hungry, Kennedy looks at the clock. It's three already? The time has flown by and she's out of pictures and has used most of her magazine clippings too. The door is covered top to bottom save for a border around the collage that she plans to paint with a flowering vine of some kind. She'll save that and the mirror bits for another day.

The phone rings and it's Willow, asking if Kennedy and Sarina are having a beach fire tonight.

"No, it's changed to tomorrow because Sarina can't go."

"Okay, great. What are you doing today?"

"Stuff," says Kennedy, mad at Willow for last night and now mad at herself for telling Willow about tomorrow. She doesn't particularly want her around Colin again.

"Uh, okay." Willow sounds more confused than hurt. "See you tomorrow, then."

After cleaning up collage scraps, Kennedy goes upstairs for some lunch. Tory, still in her pyjamas, is watching a movie from the fort she's made out of dining-room chairs and an assortment of blankets and towels, while an army of stuffed animals has overtaken the couch in the living room. Liam is on the computer and Mom is nowhere to be seen.

"Do you have any idea when Judith and Colin are expected back?" she asks Liam.

"Missing Colin, are we?" teases Liam.

"No. Are you?"

"He's not my type. I prefer straight hair, five-ten-ish, separate eyebrows."

"Colin does not have a unibrow."

"Didn't think you'd noticed."

"Oh, shut up."

"I have to say, Colin seems like kind of a jerk."

Kennedy starts at this accusation, mostly because she's always thought of Liam as a pretty decent judge of people.

"Liam," Mom says, coming in from the deck, where she's obviously been listening, "I think Colin's going through a hard time right now, so just be nice."

"What do you mean, hard time?" Kennedy recalls Judith's scolding voice talking about "facing things at home."

"Oh, being rebellious, directionless. That sort of thing."

It sounds to Kennedy as if Mom knows more than she's willing to say.

"What? Did his ego get so big it burst and blew up a building?" says Liam and proceeds to point at random objects with his finger — the TV, the coffee table, the cat — and make explosion sounds. "Pakow, pakow, pakow."

Kennedy thinks she can smell pot on Mom's breath and looks at her more closely.

"Is your movie almost over, Tory?" asks Mom. "I want to put on some music."

By the time Kennedy's made herself a sandwich, the house is booming with *The Best of the Bee Gees*. She peeks into the living room to see Mom dancing around with her eyes closed, shoulders rolling, fingers snapping out the beat. Tory, naked except for her underwear, is spinning on her bum on an old album cover. Other album covers litter the floor like stepping stones. Kennedy attempts to eat and read at the kitchen table but the music forces her out to the deck. She can't stand the lead singer's high-pitched voice. He sounds like what she imagines a castrato would sound like.

Outside it is warmer than normal, the air heavy and still, almost muggy, which is unusual for Victoria. She flips to the page where Mr. Bennet, having returned from London without having found Lydia, has received an urgent letter from Elizabeth's uncle. The letter states that Lydia has been found and will soon be married. The disconcerting part of the letter, in Mr. Bennet's view, is how little a dowry he's being asked to provide. He wonders, with shame, what impossible sum Elizabeth's uncle must have put out. *"Wickham's a fool,"* says Mr. Bennet, *"if he takes her with a farthing less than ten thousand pounds."*

"Ten thousand pounds! Heaven forbid! How is half such a sum to be repaid?" asks Elizabeth. It is only later that Elizabeth learns it was Mr. Darcy who ferreted out Wickham and made arrangements for the marriage. And that the money paid to Wickham had come from his own pocket.

Kennedy looks up from her book to see a taxi pulling into the drive. Elliot? thinks Kennedy. What is he doing here? No, she's wrong. Colin's gloriously tousled blond head steps from the car, followed by Judith.

"Colin," she calls down, a piece of tomato spewing embarrassingly from her lips.

He looks up to the deck and waves, smiling his brilliant smile. God, he's gorgeous, she thinks, finding it hard to swallow. She hurries inside to put the rest of her sandwich in the fridge. The stereo's blaring *Saturday Night Fever* now, but Mom's no longer dancing. Instead she's in the kitchen intensely focused on measuring Rice Krispies into a pot on the stove. Kennedy can smell the heady sweetness of melted marshmallows. Tory, still unclothed, is rubbing butter-smeared hands along the bottom of a baking pan.

"We're making Krispie squares," says Tory over the music, smiling as she pops a chocolate chip in her mouth. Her hair sticks out from her head at odd angles. "We're putting in raisins and choco-chips." She smiles and her teeth are smudged brown with chocolate.

"Mom, Tory's stuffing herself with chocolate chips," says Kennedy.

"Don't eat them all, Tory," says Mom lazily. "We want to put them in our squares."

"Go away." Tory glares at Kennedy and pops another chip in her mouth.

Kennedy shakes her head. "I'm gone."

She passes Judith on the stairs and asks how she enjoyed whale watching.

"It was bumpy," says Judith, rubbing her back. "We were in one of those small raft things with a giant motor on the back. Never need to do that again."

Kennedy and her family did the whale thing when they first came to Victoria, back when Mom thought it was educational. Pounding the water at high speed in a Zodiac was the most thrilling part.

She finds Colin in her bedroom, of all places, sifting through her music collection.

"Hey, who said you could come in here?" she teases.

"Sorry, just felt like we should put on some music down here. Drown out that." He points to the ceiling.

"Yeah. My mom gets into music when my dad's away." She leaves out the smoking pot part.

"Good for her," he says. "Saw a whole family pod of killer whales." He flicks through CDs. "And two grey whales. It was pretty spectacular."

"Your mom seemed to dislike the boat ride."

"That was the best part, slapping over the waves and getting sprayed."

"I know, I loved that."

"What a lot of chick music," he says.

"You could try the radio."

"Good idea."

She watches his hands fiddle with the tuner. Hands that were holding her just last night.

"Boy, I'd love a joint right about now," he sighs.

Kennedy pictures the tin on the kitchen shelf with the shaving baby on it. "I could get you some," she blurts.

The way Colin looks at her, Kennedy feels seriously cool for the first time in her life.

"Really?" He stops and reaches out his hand for her to take. She takes it and he pulls her to him, kissing her head through her hair.

"I could," she says as he lifts her hair and bends over to kiss the side of her neck. One hand smooths down the line of her ribs to her waist. Then he stops and playfully pushes her away.

"Well, go on then," he says. "But do come back."

Kennedy starts out the door. "Back in ten minutes," she says.

What am I doing? she asks herself on the way upstairs. Stealing from her mom is what she's doing. Of course, if she takes just a little bit, Mom probably won't notice. All she needs is enough for one small joint. She'll have to take a couple of papers too. Hell, if Mom's going to keep it in the house, what can she expect?

A haggard-looking Judith is sitting at the kitchen table, drinking coffee and telling Mom about the whale-watching tour. A plate of Rice Krispie squares sits on the table in front of them. Mom's staring at her, not responding, just eating a square, a strand of marshmallow goo connecting her hand to her mouth. Tory's just finishing one and reaching for another, her face and hands a disaster.

"Tory, did you have any lunch?" Kennedy asks.

"Krispie squares."

"Mom, did Tory have any lunch?" she asks, interrupting Judith.

"No. Can you give her a glass of milk for me, please?"

Eyeing the tin on top of the cupboard, Kennedy opens the fridge. "You guys should sit outside on the deck. It's really nice out. Super warm."

Judith and Mom don't move. Kennedy pours the milk and then deftly removes the plate of Rice Krispie squares from the table and starts to take it out to the deck. "Come, sit out here," she says again, louder this time. "The air smells great."

As Mom starts in about "whales having no privacy to give birth, much less mate," she mindlessly follows the plate of squares. Judith and Tory follow.

Once they're settled on the deck, Kennedy slips back into the kitchen. She grabs the tin and a sandwich baggie and takes them into the bathroom. She puts just enough pot and two papers into the baggie, then hurries to replace the tin among the others. She hears Mom talking outside. She's onto the cougar situation.

Colin is lying on her bed, flipping through a *Cosmo Girl* magazine Kennedy borrowed from Sarina. Some raunchy punk band is screaming on the radio.

"Hey," she says, feeling as cool as she sounds.

"Any luck?" His face is eager, almost desperate-looking.

"What's it to you?" she teases, enjoying the moment.

"Well, did you or didn't you?" he asks, frowning.

She pulls the bag from her pocket.

"All right," he says, smiling again. "Where did you get it?"

"My secret." She hands it over.

"This all?"

"I just took enough for one joint," she says.

"One razor-thin joint," he corrects.

"Well, I can put it back," she says, feeling insulted now.

"No, no, sorry to sound greedy," he says, changing his tune. "Come sit down."

He licks the two papers together and lays them out on her *Pride and Prejudice* book.

"A movie of this book came out in England some time back," he says.

"Yeah, I know. I'm sure it wasn't nearly as good as the last one."

"There's a last one?" He sprinkles the pot onto the papers, every last green bit, carefully rolls it up and licks it closed. Putting the joint between his lips, he pulls a lighter from his pocket.

"In here?" says Kennedy.

"Out there?" Colin asks out of the corner of his mouth. He points up to the deck and the muffled voices of their mothers.

"I guess it's safer," she agrees, and gets up to lock the door.

He lights up and they pass it back and forth, Kennedy alert to where Colin's knee touches her thigh. She takes only small drags so she won't cough as much this time. When it burns down to practically nothing, Colin pops the tiny butt in his mouth.

"Ick," she says, staring.

"Yum," he says, and leaning over her, presses her down on the bed.

She doesn't stop him this time, but kisses him back, running her hands over his hair like she's always wanted to. An old David Usher song comes on the radio, the one that's mixed up with that amazing operatic piece. Kennedy feels reduced to only ears and skin as Colin's hands start roaming her exposed waist. He stops, pops back on his heels and peels his shirt over his head. She breathes in the sight of his muscled chest and then he's back on top of her, kissing her, the warmth of his chest penetrating her thin tank top. He rolls off to one side and his hand slips under her top and over her bra. She can't help but moan softly as his mouth slips away from hers. He's lifting her shirt, one hand expertly undoing her bra. Then his mouth is on her breast! The feeling is so heavenly that she has to bite her lips to keep from screaming. He presses his hips against her thigh, and she can tell he has a hard-on. God, she doesn't want to go there, but then he's moving off her leg and his mouth is continuing down her body.

She reaches for his arms to pull him back up.

"Colin ..."

"It's okay, you're going to like this," he says, winking both his eyes at her.

"But ..."

"Shhh ..." he hushes and softly kisses her belly button.

Kennedy's head falls back on the bed, unsure, and she closes her eyes as he undoes her shorts. Then he's pulling them off along with her thong. Her breath catches in her throat. His mouth is down there! She can't begin to think about what it is he's doing, but the sensations are so intense, so wildly amazing that she feels like laughing and crying both. She grinds her teeth together as the muscles of her body seem to tense up one by one. She's going to burst out of her skin if he doesn't stop. Something lets go and a tiny fire ricochets up her spine, igniting layers of nerves an ocean deep.

"Oh my god," escapes her lips, her face flushing with heat.

The sensations start to subside and her hips drop onto the bed. She hadn't even noticed that she'd raised them.

"Hey," comes Colin's soft voice as he slides back up to her face. "Did that feel good?"

She just looks at him with hollow eyes, then grabs him around the neck. Could this be what love feels like? He snuggles up beside her and Kennedy starts kissing his face all over. Then there it is again, his hard-on against her leg. She's eternally grateful for the pleasure he just gave her but really hopes he doesn't expect the same from her.

"Colin," she says in a mousy voice, "I don't want to have sex or anything."

"Yeah, okay," he mumbles, pressing harder. "How about a hand job?"

Before she can answer, he undoes his pants and pushes Kennedy's hand down his boxers.

PAIN #24: BEING CLUELESS

Why don't they teach you anything truly useful in sex ed?

She takes tentative hold of him and Colin's hips start thrusting, mildly at first and then bucking like a bull out of its pen. She closes her eyes and holds on tighter.

"Up and down," he hisses through clenched teeth, and she tries to oblige but it's hard when he's moving like he is.

Then he's clasping his hand over hers to work their two hands down and up, together.

She ventures a peek at his face. His jutting jaw makes him look gnomish and grotesque. Did she look like that? She shuts her eyes and holds on. His breath huffs harder in her ear, then abruptly stops as his hand freezes over hers. His breath releases into her ear in one long hot rush.

Colin slowly loosens his hand grip and she does the same. Then he falls back on the pillow, his chest lifting and falling, working to catch his breath.

"Give us a rag, will you?" he says, his eyes closing.

18

PAIN #25: FEELING ABANDONED

Kennedy was expecting, after what they did, that she and Colin would go out together tonight. To the movies, maybe, or dinner. A real date. But Colin said he wanted to hit a few bars downtown, said she'd never be able to get in.

"Sorry there, girl," he said with a squeeze of her arm, and left right after dinner. Order-in pizza, that is, since Mom's too lazy to cook. Mom left then too, went to a rehearsal, or so she said. And Judith was going to visit an old neighbour from her Victoria days. That left her, Tory and Liam to pass the night together. But if she was honest with herself, she didn't mind. This afternoon was a lot to process, Colin was a lot to process, and in a way she was grateful to be alone with her thoughts. At least now she knows what her mom's on about. Orgasms are incredible. Holy. Though not altogether pretty.

Kennedy lets Tory help glue the mirror pieces onto her picture collage and then, as Kennedy paints in a border, Tory paints her cast with lopsided flowers and egg-headed smiley faces.

Kennedy doesn't lay eyes on Colin again until the next morning. Asleep in the rec room, he must have come home late again, since she never even heard him come in. She herself had stayed up until midnight, which was when her mom sauntered in.

"Where were you?" Kennedy asked.

"We went out for a beer after rehearsal. I tried to call but the line was busy."

Kennedy didn't remember being on the phone. Was Liam even up? She had to wonder if Mom was telling the truth and should have asked her then and there. Are you cheating on Dad? Again? But it felt too weird to ask after what she herself had been doing that afternoon. But *she* was allowed. She was supposed to be "exploring her sexuality," to quote Mom. Kennedy wasn't the one who was married with three kids.

As she passes Colin in bed that morning, she thinks about snuggling in beside him, pulling his arms over her and feeling his warmth against her back. But then thinks twice. What if he got hard again? That part was really awkward, to say the least. Besides, her period's due today, so no way. Upstairs, she goes directly to the computer to check in with her friends. She hopes Sarina is online. Is dying to tell her what happened. They've never talked about orgasms before. Has Sarina had one? Maybe she's had all sorts. How varied do they get, she wonders.

Upstairs, the house is quiet. Everyone seems to be out. She remembers that Tory was going for a play date at her friend Sasha's today and Liam's probably at Sam's, who's back from wherever it was he went. Mom and Judith must have gone for a walk or something. Alone in the house with Colin again. The phone rings and, suddenly worried that Colin might wake up and expect something of her, she rushes to answer it. She hopes it's Sarina.

"Hello?"

"Hello. Is Kennedy there?"

"Speaking."

"It's Elliot."

"Oh, hi." What's he calling her for?

"I just wanted to ask how Tory's leg was doing?"

"Oh, fine. Doesn't seem to hurt her anymore. And thanks again for all your help the other night."

"Not a problem."

There's an awkward silence and Kennedy can't think of what to say.

"I was also wondering if you might want to go to the opera with me. *La Bohème* is playing next month. I remember you said you liked singing."

He's asking her out? Elliot? What does she say?

"I've always wanted to go see an opera," she says, which is the truth.

"I've never been either, but I've heard it's pretty amazing."

That was honest of him, she thinks, liking the idea that it would be new for both of them. If she says yes, though, will he think she likes him? ... like that?

"It's awfully expensive, isn't it?"

"I have a friend who isn't using his season tickets."

Another friend. At least he won't be spending his own money. She really would love to go. "I'll have to ask my parents."

"Sure."

"So, I'll have to get back to you."

"Fine. Do you want my number?"

Not really, she thinks. "Okay."

After they hang up, Kennedy stands in the middle of the kitchen. Jordan suddenly seems to belong to another time and planet. Elliot? That's too weird. She always felt he thought of her as beneath him, as just a kid. They could just be friends. And maybe that's all that Elliot's thinking anyway. She doesn't have to read anything more into it.

Sarina is online and in a great mood.

hi sar. how wz pender?

excellent. Got Mom n Dad talking. they'd let all this resentment stew n never really talked it out. amazing

. *thats so great*

hes still moving which is sad. but they joked about dating. isnt that romantic? anyway, things dont feel so cold round here. so im pretty happy

Kennedy suddenly doesn't want to tell Sarina about Colin. Not online anyway. What if Zak the perv is listening?

elliot just called n asked me 2 go 2 the opera with hm

really? the opera?

weird eh? i mean hes nice n all but i figured he considered us beneath hm

hes nerdy but handsome. maybe he doesnt hav many friends. or maybe ur some sort of guy magnet thes days. whats up with colin?

tell u when i cu. wen should we do the beach fire at Mount Doug? 5?

sure. i'll com to your place. u bring drink. i'll get food.

i invited chase. willow called, said u invited her n amber. shes going 2 try n score som drink

Willow, thinks Kennedy. *whatever. mind if i com over now?*

no, cu soon

Kennedy's about to log off when the message light flashes at her.

hi ken, zak here. hoping to run into you sometime. i hear you like older guys. true?

Kennedy exits as quickly as she can. She pictures Creepy Guy and the hairs on the back of her neck stand on end. What if he is dangerous? And what if he knows where she lives? She's grateful she's not alone in the house right now. And Willow aside, she's glad lots of people are coming tonight. She'll remind Sarina to bring her cell.

Kennedy leaves a note for Colin about the beach fire. She doesn't really want to be here, just the two of them, when he wakes up. On the other hand, she can't wait to be with him tonight around all her friends. Though they'll have to be discreet because of Jordan and all. She's definitely going to have to break up with Jordan when he gets home. In all honesty, she has to admit she doesn't like him "enough," and it's just not fair to him. And now she's probably going on a quasi date with Elliot! To the opera, which is pretty cool. She doesn't even think her parents have been to an opera. She wonders if she'll have to dress up? Don't women wear gowns to the opera? Black tie for men? If only she were going with Colin. Now that would be romantic.

Walking to Sarina's house, she can't help eyeing the trees and bushes by the side of the road. She searches the face of the driver of an approaching car. When she sees it's not Creepy Guy, she feels silly and relaxes her guard.

Sarina is the cheeriest Kennedy's seen her in months and she can't help but tell her what happened yesterday with Colin. Not the second part, just what happened to her. She doesn't go into too much detail, but does mention the end result. Sarina laughs and gives Kennedy a hug.

"Amazing that our bodies do that, isn't it?" she says, her eyes shining. "I knew he liked you. Willow will be so jealous. Last night on the way home, she said he was the hottest guy she'd ever met."

"'Course we all know about Willow's taste in men," says Kennedy, secretly pleased.

"And now Elliot's after you too, eh? Chalk up two points for Kennedy," Sarina says, making two check marks in the air.

"But I feel so bad about Jordan."

"You going to break up with him?"

"I have to now. Did I tell you that Colin invited me to visit him in England?"

"No way."

"Way."

"He must like you a lot."

"I guess."

Kennedy calls first before heading home, just to make sure Mom or someone else besides Colin is there. Mom answers, music raging in the background. Is she stoned again?

"Colin's gone out," Mom says, "but he said to tell you he'd be back at five. Something about a beach fire?"

"Yeah, thanks Mom. I'll be home soon." She hangs up.

"Colin's coming," she smiles.

"Coming?" says Sarina.

"Stop that." Kennedy laughs.

"Should be fun, with or without Creepy Guy Zak showing his ugly face."

Having picked out the first part of the love-song medley from *Moulin Rouge*, Kennedy is singing in her room. She's purposely left the window open a crack, just in case Colin comes home. She wants to impress him, make him fall for her that much more. She thinks she could do it now — sing solo in front of people, that is. She imagines that orgasm having pushed her over an edge of self-consciousness. At least she thinks she could sing in front of one person anyway. For starters.

Singing with what feels like her entire being, Kennedy closes her eyes and pictures an audience before her, filled with friends and family. As she sustains the final note of the song, the crown of her head tingling just right, she opens her eyes to a face pressed up against her window. It startles her and she jumps clear of her seat. For a second she thought it was Creepy Guy.

"What's all the screaming about?" Colin says through

the opened window, and her stomach contracts in embarrassment. "Just kidding there, Kennedy, but hey, when's this do tonight?"

He's dismissed her singing altogether. She feels idiotic. She looks at the clock.

"Sarina's coming in about ten minutes. Then we're meeting a few other friends at the beach."

"A regular party," he says, lingering at the window and lighting up a cigarette. He sounds spaced out. Stoned?

He wanders from the window and Kennedy quickly puts away her keyboard. She couldn't really sound that bad, could she? Maybe he didn't like her choice of music. In any case, she's mortified that he's heard her at all. Singing both parts of a duet at that. By herself. He probably thinks she's a total dork.

Sarina arrives right on time wearing a backpack full of hot dogs, buns and s'more makings: graham crackers, marshmallows and Hershey bars. Sarina can be so generous. Kennedy goes upstairs to get cans of pop and to fill a couple of water bottles. The stairs are littered with Tory's stuffed animals and the couch is overturned.

"Kendy, look at my fort," calls Tory, sticking her head out from behind a sheet draped over the end of the couch.

"Cool," says Kennedy, continuing into the kitchen.

The kitchen is a little cleaner; at least the dishes are done.

"Kennedy," calls Mom from what sounds like her bedroom.

What now? thinks Kennedy, heading down the hall.

No, I'm not babysitting so you can go out and do whatever it is you do.

"Come in and shut the door." Mom's tone is serious.

Next to her on the bed sits the tin with the picture of the shaving baby on it. Mom's hiding place for her dope. Oh shit, did she miss that little bit?

"I have to ask if you know what's in this can," says Mom.

"Well," Kennedy stammers, "I was looking for chocolate one day, a couple of weeks ago, and looked in it, yes." She tries her best to hold her mom's eye without blinking or looking away.

"And did you happen to take what was in it?"

"It's gone?" Kennedy thinks to ask before confessing.

Mom lifts out the empty bag. "Yes. It's gone."

"I didn't Mom, I swear," she can say in all honesty.

"Must be Colin," sighs Mom, shaking her head. "Such a difficult kid. Didn't mean to accuse you, Kennedy. Just had to ask you first. And," Mom looks sheepish now, "I just smoke it every now and again. Very rarely." She smiles a kind of sad smile. "Like to pretend I'm young and care-free again, I guess."

Kennedy feels like crying suddenly. She's not sure why.

"Judith says Colin's been nothing but trouble since he turned fifteen," says Mom. "He dropped out of school before finishing his last year, won't get a job, and she told me today why he can't drive. He didn't forget his licence, it was taken away. Impaired driving charge. He ran into a lamp post. Apparently there was a girl in the passenger seat who's now in the hospital with severe neck and shoulder injuries. Her parents are suing. Colin's father, what with his government connections, was able to keep Colin out of jail.

It's why they're here in Canada. Judith had to take him out of the country until things cooled down. Imagine."

Kennedy's shocked but tries not to show it.

"A little time in jail might have done him some good," continues her mom. "His parents don't seem to be able to handle him." She runs a hand through the little hair she has left. "Judith's completely stressed out and has a bit of a drinking problem, by the looks of it," Mom adds, looking defeated.

"I was wondering about that," says Kennedy.

"I've been trying to find a way to talk to her about it. But she's pretty defensive. Just might slip an AA brochure into her suitcase when she goes. But sorry to keep you, sweetheart. You go on. Just don't be getting into any cars with Colin. And if you see my marijuana around ..." She hesitates. "Oh, I don't need it. Gives me a headache now, actually." She laughs and waves Kennedy away.

"Mom," says Kennedy, thinking this might be the right time. "Do you love Dad?"

"Of course I do. More than anything. Except for you kids. Your father's my best friend and my anchor in life. A spouse *should* be your best friend, you know," she adds, slipping into advice mode.

"Does Dad know you smoke pot?"

"Oh sure. We don't keep secrets from each other. That would be too much work. But because he doesn't like smoking in general, I only do it when he's out of town."

Okay, thinks Kennedy, do it now. Just say it. She takes a big breath.

"Have you ever cheated on Dad?"

Mom looks sideways at her.

"No, Kennedy. I haven't. I'll admit I considered it once. But knew I'd only regret it afterward and couldn't go through with it. The fantasy of love is one thing, reality is another." Mom sighs. "You don't go ruining a good thing. And they don't come any better than your dad."

Kennedy doesn't need to hear any more.

"But why would you ask such a thing?" asks Mom, stopping her.

Kennedy was hoping she wouldn't ask that.

"Uh ... I guess because ... Sarina's folks are splitting up and ..."

"Oh, sweetie, and poor Sarina. That's terrible news. You don't have to worry about your dad and me. We're lifers, I'm afraid."

Kennedy smiles gratefully. "So, I guess I'll see you later." She opens the door to leave, hears Tory talking to herself in her room and feels a sudden rush of affection toward her.

"Is Colin being a gentleman?" Mom asks, as if it's her turn now.

"Sure. He's pretty nice." Kennedy can't share anything more with her. Not yet.

"He's older than you and your friends, and a lot more experienced ... so just make sure no one gets ... hurt."

"Sure. You don't worry, either. And sorry about the missing pot."

Mom shrugs and blows Kennedy a quick kiss.

Kennedy's head is suddenly filled with way too much information. She grabs the pop and water and stuffs them in her backpack along with a sweater, flashlight and some matches. Impaired driving charge? He doesn't seem very remorseful about that girl. Was she his girlfriend? Could he really have stolen Mom's pot? Well, he took Dad's beers, so why wouldn't he? She wonders how many more of those beers he might have snitched?

Colin is outside with Sarina. He has Sarina laughing about something.

"Colin," Kennedy says as they start walking. "Did you steal some pot from us?"

Colin doesn't respond right away. "From us?"

"From the kitchen."

"I happened to come across some, yes. But I assumed it was yours, and —"

"And you didn't ask, but just took it?" She's angry now. How can he feel anything for her if he does things like this?

"Sorry, Kennedy. I would have asked, but you weren't home. Then I forgot about it. Don't look so ticked. I was certainly going to pay you for what I smoke and," he fishes in his pocket, "give the rest back."

He sounds so sincere she doesn't know what to think. She takes the bag and zips it into a pocket of her pack.

"Though it might be a good night for such things," he says and slides his arm around her waist.

His hand feels wonderfully warm on her skin but she pulls away. "I wish you had asked, that's all."

She has to wonder if she knows this Colin person at all.

19

Colin does most of the talking as they walk through the woods toward the beach, going on about Elliot and school sports back in grade seven. "He was pathetic, really, volleyball, basketball, soccer, you name it. He was our goalie for soccer but only because nobody else wanted to do it. I remember the time the ball hit him square between the eyes, a terribly close-range kick. He was counting blades of grass or something, totally unawares, and this ball smacked him brutally hard. He was knocked out cold and fell over right on the ball. Saving the goal!" Colin's loud laugh is quickly swallowed up by the trees.

"Elliot seems like a nice guy," says Sarina, glancing at Kennedy.

"If you like brainy types with no sense of humour," Colin says as he picks up a rock and heaves it at a tree.

Shut up, Kennedy wants to say. You don't know Elliot. For the first time, she thinks that it's Colin who's jealous of Elliot and not the other way around.

When they reach the beach, it's high tide, the sandy area narrowed to just a few metres wide. Bounded by woods, there is only one clear pathway down from the parking lot. If Creepy Guy comes down here, he'll be impossible to miss, thinks Kennedy.

"Look," says Sarina, pointing.

The sun is shining on San Juan Island across the strait and Mount Baker floats godlike in the distance. It's an impressive sight. Kennedy tries to breathe in the mountain's serene strength — something she can use about now.

She, Sarina and Colin half-drag, half-roll a couple of driftwood logs around the black smear of what was someone else's campfire. They gather sticks and dried leaves for kindling and hunt for the right-sized driftwood for burning. Colin continues his small talk with Sarina and avoids Kennedy. Confused about a lot of things now, Kennedy prefers he keep his distance.

"So who's this man we're looking out for?" asks Colin. "A psycho-killer, is he?"

"Let's hope not," says Sarina. "We think it might be this dumpy, middle-aged guy who was watching us play tennis."

"Distinguishing features?"

"None to speak of. Has a black dog and wears a baseball cap."

"Here comes a dog and baseball cap now," says Colin. "Wrong colour dog, though."

They look up to see Chase and his dog Mocha coming down the beach. Kennedy's glad he brought Mocha — dogs feel like safety. Willow and Amber are following behind and Willow is dressed in another skimpy, busty outfit.

"Hey, Chase," waves Sarina, and he nods back. "He's so cute," she adds under her breath, but Kennedy catches it. Maybe, after all these years, Sarina's finally coming around.

"Is that the girl from the other night?" Colin asks.

"Yeah, Willow," says Sarina.

"Willow," he repeats to himself, and Kennedy rolls her eyes.

As Kennedy sets the dry leaves afire, Sarina introduces Chase to Colin. Pulling ciders from her pack, Willow is all smiles.

"I brought booze," she announces, looking straight at Colin.

"This may be more fun than I thought," says Colin, giving Willow one of his charming half-smiles.

Chase throws a stick in the water and Mocha goes in after it.

"Maybe we should all have a swim later," suggests Colin. "When the sun goes down."

"Water's pretty cold," says Amber, "and we didn't bring our suits."

"We won't need them if it's dark," says Willow coyly.

An hour later and still no sign of Creepy Guy, everyone has been into the cider except Kennedy. She feels like staying sober, and focuses on keeping the fire going. Chase is unusually quiet, deferring to the older male perhaps, and talks privately to Sarina whenever the opportunity arises. Kennedy knows that Chase never liked Willow much and that he finds Amber irritating.

Colin is entertaining whoever will listen with stories of living in various parts of the world. Kennedy is having trouble believing that he lost three dogs to snakebites in Australia, was chased by a baboon in Africa and was mugged on the streets of New York in broad daylight. They may very well be true, but she's having trouble believing him altogether. Willow laughs at everything that issues from Colin's cushiony lips, and he returns the favour with what seem to Kennedy to be more and more seductive smiles. Amber laughs at his stories too, an echo later than Willow, but Colin ignores her.

Why don't you tell us why you're travelling with Mummy, Kennedy feels like saying. She can't believe how little he seems to care that she's upset with him. What with all the attention he's paying Willow, he probably wouldn't even notice if she got up and left.

Sarina brings out the hot dogs and tells everyone to hunt down a cooking stick.

"I can't believe him," Kennedy says to Sarina as the others go search the woods for branches.

"He sure is flirting up Willow."

"What an idiot I am." She snaps off a branch. "I just want to leave."

"Don't, Kennedy. Just talk to him. Tell him you're upset. He'll stop."

"I wonder."

"You need to speak up for yourself," says Sarina, with a nudge in Colin's direction, and Kennedy knows Sarina's right. She can't expect people to read her mind.

"Yeah, okay," she says.

She heads up into the woods, tripping over the perfect

cooking stick. Picking it up, she hears Colin's distinctive voice. "No, there's nothing between us. Besides," his voice deepens, "Kennedy's just a kid compared to you."

Kennedy whips the air with her stick, does an about-face and storms back to the fire. A minute later, Willow comes flouncing out of the woods waving her branch, Colin trailing behind, her hair a whole lot messier than five minutes ago. Kennedy stares hard at Colin but he won't even look her way. They all put hot dogs on their branches and start rotating them above the fire. Colin squeezes himself between Amber and Willow. Why did she ever think he was sincere about her? How blind could she be?

"Wieners on a stick," says Willow, and Colin gives her a look. The look.

Though Kennedy can't tell for sure, it looks as if Colin's bare foot may be touching Willow's under the sand. Kennedy can't believe it. Go back to England, she thinks angrily.

"Kennedy!" yells Amber. "Your stick."

Kennedy's wiener is on fire. She plunges it even deeper in the flames.

"Have another," says Sarina.

"I'm not hungry."

Sarina has brought chips, buns and condiments too, and everyone else digs in. Kennedy takes a handful of chips but ends up throwing most of them to Mocha.

"Well, this pervert fellow seems to be missing the party," Colin says to Kennedy.

"Or maybe he's spying on us, watching us eat," says Amber, her brow wrinkling.

"We could branch out in the woods and hunt him down," says Colin, obviously not taking Creepy Guy seriously.

He stands up, tossing the last quarter of his hot dog in the fire. Mocha whines sadly. "We could break up into teams."

"I'll go," says Willow, standing up next to him.

"Okay, me and Willow," he says as casually as he can. "Any other teams?"

He looks at Kennedy and she glares back. His eyes quickly move on to Chase beside her. Sarina looks from Kennedy to Colin.

"I don't want to," interrupts Amber, reaching for another hot dog.

"Fine, fine. We'll scour the woods and you guys watch the beach. But if you hear us cry for help, do come running," he says, and Willow nods in agreement. "But Kennedy," he adds in his most silken voice, "how about we all smoke a little of your weed first. No point in being greedy, don't you —"

"What?" Kennedy nearly screams. "I can't believe you," she says, surging off her log to barge between him and Willow, knocking his shoulder back. Fuelled with anger, she sprints up into the tree line and keeps going.

"Kennedy, wait," Sarina calls, which only makes Kennedy move faster.

She can't talk right now. She just wants to be alone, pervert in the woods or not. She's ashamed of her stupidity and couldn't care less what happens to her. Branches whip her face, one catching her hair with a yank. She doesn't stop and several hairs rip from their roots.

"Kennedy!" Sarina's voice again, obviously following her.

There's a semblance of a path off to the right and Kennedy claws her way through the brush toward it, hurrying away from Sarina's voice. Elliot was right not to trust Colin, she thinks. Colin's the jerk, not Elliot. She breaks into a run, branches scratching her arms and legs. She hears Sarina calling, her voice smaller now, farther away. This path must lead up to the road, she figures, then she'll hike the mountain and down the other side toward home. Kennedy hears rustling ahead of her and sees a flash of white through the leaves. What? She stops. Could it be him? She quickly steps off the path and behind a tree.

Her blood pounds in her head, a combination of anger and nerves mixing messages. If it's Creepy Guy, she tells herself, she'll wait for him to pass, then run to the phone at the bathroom area. Do you need a quarter to dial 911? The crunch of footsteps comes closer. She pictures Creepy Guy's cheap white shirt. Maybe he wears the same thing every day.

A whispery voice. More than one person? Maybe he's crazy and talks to himself. Oh no, if his dog's with him the dog will sniff her out. She wants to run now, in the other direction or back down to the beach. Too late. He's coming around the corner. Kennedy stands with her back glued to the tree, not daring to breathe. Unsure whether her body is completely covered by the tree trunk, she shifts her feet just enough to accidentally snap a branch loudly in two with her heel. Shit. The footsteps stop. She expects a dog to start barking crazily. The steps start again, a slower pace. In her direction? She has to look. Oh god. She moves her head, ever so slowly around the tree ...

"Ahhhh!" they all scream at once.

"Jeez, Kennedy," says a breathless Liam. "What are you doing here?"

"Me?" she yells freely now, unleashing the anger she

couldn't with Colin. "What the hell are you and Sam doing here?"

"Uh, we were sneaking up on you guys?" says Liam, sheepish in the face of his sister's rage.

"What for, you freaks?"

"So that you'd think Zak Smith was after you," offers Sam with a dumb smile.

"What sort of stupid logic is that? He may be in these very woods as we speak and you're making a joke of it?" She pushes past to keep walking. She's afraid now the others have heard them and will come after her.

"We are Zak Smith," says Liam to her retreating back.

"What?" she stops to face them.

"It *was* a joke," explains Sam. "Liam sent those messages from my house."

Kennedy just stares at him, then shakes her head. "What about Sarah across the street?"

"Made that up," said Liam.

"More deception!" she yells at the trees. "Perfect. I must be the biggest sucker on the face of the planet."

She starts to run now. Leaving the boys behind, leaving slimeball Colin behind.

"Sorry, Kennedy," she hears Liam call out. His apology sounds almost sincere, but what does she know about sincerity?

She reaches the road, rushes between passing cars and finds a narrow path heading up the steep mountainside. Refusing to slow down, Kennedy is winded and her left calf is starting to cramp. She doesn't care. The physical pain helps focus her confusion and anger. She's so dumb. First Colin and now Liam. She hates dishonesty more than anything.

How do you know what's real if there's no honesty?

She tears at branches, hauling herself forward. Of course she allowed herself to be deceived. Colin was smarmy and selfish from day one. Even Liam could see it. So she's not even honest with herself. She doesn't want to think anymore and moves faster, her thighs aching now too. As she nears the top she slows, her breath coming hard and fast. She remembers Colin's heaving breath yesterday and shuts down the image. She stops at the top, giving her muscles and lungs a rest. Her body wants to sit down among the Garry oaks and take in the view, the sunset, but then her brain will start up and she just doesn't want to think.

She starts downhill. She knows this path and that it will eventually lead home. But does she want to go there? Judith will be there, another liar. And if Colin does or doesn't come home tonight, either way it's painful and she'd just rather not be around.

Down in the tall trees with their high green canopy, the path has darkened and the air is cool against her sweat-soaked skin. She could spend the night at Sarina's or maybe haul a camping mattress out to Tory's treehouse. She doesn't want to lay eyes on Colin ever again.

The sun's going down and a green twilight presses in around her, the kind of light that makes your eyes feel fuzzy, as if the world is breaking down into floating particles of light. A stoned feeling, thinks Kennedy. No one walking their dogs at this late hour, no hikers trudging the paths. It's amazing how quiet the forest is, how eerily still despite the fact that it's full of life — birds, squirrels, rabbits, raccoons. Not even a leaf is moving. Kennedy remembers the flashlight she left behind in her pack.

She could use it before long. She also remembers the pot. Colin's probably stolen it again unless Sarina somehow stopped him. She imagines him going for her pack, Sarina grabbing it away from him, Colin knocking her down and Chase jumping on him, landing a few fast punches while Mocha bites into Colin's leg. For an instant, she feels a little better.

Up ahead is the main path that eventually leads into their subdivision. She's in no hurry, really, except for the fading light, and she stops to breathe in the peaceful stillness, hoping it will settle her thoughts. Kennedy suddenly senses a presence, the faintest feeling of being watched, of being studied. Creepy Guy, she thinks, her breath halting, then remembers there is no Creepy Guy. Expecting to see Liam again, she turns around ready with a sneer on her face. Nothing.

She continues to walk, but the feeling of being watched stops her again. There may be other perverts, real ones. She looks behind her again. No one there. She looks up at the dark silhouettes of leafy trees to her right, then to her left. Holy shit! She stumbles backward, nearly falling. Not five steps away, perched on the lowest branch of an oak tree and staring at her with eyes that glow yellow in the dimming light, is a real live, muscle-and-teeth cougar.

"Oh," is all she manages to say.

Kennedy's adrenalin roars into overdrive. It takes all her will to deny the instinct to turn and run. Keep your wits, she hears a little voice say in her head. It's the ones who panic that lose their lives, she remembers someone saying once — a park ranger? Dad? She spies a large stick lying near the edge of the path and quickly bends to grab it.

She lifts it high over her head. Shakes it. Her mind races to remember what else you're supposed to do. Look them in the eye, yell, sing. Whatever you do, don't turn your back and don't run.

"Go away," she yells in a shaky voice, stepping backward along the path and waving the stick in the air.

The cougar springs soundlessly to the ground and her heart hiccups in her chest.

"Go away," she tries again louder, and one golden paw steps forward.

Her yelling rings false. She's projecting her fear, her weakness. Animals can smell and taste fear, she thinks, can sense it in every fibre of their spring-loaded muscles. The cougar moves forward, keeping pace with her careful steps backward. It's a young cougar, she thinks, judging from its size. Male. She knows it's the males that get pushed out of their territory.

"Get out of here!" she yells again. "Get lost." Her voice catches and cracks in her tightening throat. Breathe, she tells herself. Breathe.

Though she's afraid to stop looking at him, she has to glance behind her to see where she's going, to not run into a tree or trip over a root. Don't trip, she tells herself. To trip is to end up prey on the ground. She has to become the dominant, more confident one, the one that deserves this territory more, that deserves to live. The main path is steps behind her now. The cougar follows her on soundless feet, his head hung low between powerful shoulders, his gaze unwavering.

"Go," she yells again, but her voice is only a sickly squeak.

Reaching the wide main path, and no longer having to check behind her, Kennedy locks eyes with the cat. Too afraid to think about being afraid, her senses become concentrated in the glow of those eyes. Honest animal eyes that hunt to kill, to fill an honest belly. These is no deception in his eyes and no fancy words coming from his mouth. His muscled shoulders roll under the golden fur as each paw leaves an imprint on the dirt.

Sing, she hears the voice in her head command. Now! A wavery humming starts up in her throat. Focused on his unblinking eyes, she starts to feel his clear and solid presence as her own. The tension in her own muscles feels no longer separate from his. The humming moves down into her chest, then widens into her belly. Sing! She takes an impossibly large breath, then, as if her diaphragm were a catapult, hurls the sound outward, hurls it into those mirror-like eyes and beyond to the forest canopy.

"Every night in my dreams, I see you, I feel you. That is how I know you go on."

Louder, says the voice.

"Far across the distance and spaces between us, you have come to show you go on."

Her body feels suddenly bigger, as if it's as large as the sound.

"Near, far, wherever you are, I believe that the heart does go on."

With each step backward, the animal steps one forward. One back, one forward, keeping the distance of two? three metres? She knows he can pounce that far in the blink of an eye, so she doesn't blink, just sings the *Titanic* song louder, sings it bigger, pushes it into those untamed eyes.

She doesn't know a lot of things, but she knows she doesn't want to die.

"Every night in my dreams, I see you, I feel you. That is how I know you go on."

She can't think of the rest of the song, so she starts over, singing louder. The words don't matter. Now she's as tall as the trees and wide as the mountain. There is power in this sound and they both understand what is being said. This animal has no difficulty distinguishing truth from lies. Who can growl the loudest? Who can care the most? Who can stand their ground the longest?

"Far across the distance and spaces between us, you have come to show you go on."

Kennedy hears a car engine in the distance. Is she nearing the parking lot? The cat hears it too and hesitates in his step.

She keeps walking, keeps claiming this territory with her voice. She shakes the stick over her head and the cougar stops. He blinks and she knows it's over — she's beaten him — but doesn't dare stop singing.

"Near, far, wherever you are, I believe that the heart does go on."

The cat turns with a low growl, whips his tail as if in surrender. He starts back up the path, then stops, his head swinging around again, eyes still watchful. She shakes her stick once more, a final threatening command, and sings even louder.

"Near, far, wherever you are ..."

Then he's gone into the trees and she stops singing. Fear rushes in to fill the sudden quiet and she turns and runs like she's never run before. Around the corner someone is coming up the path toward her.

"Kennedy," she hears, but can't see who it is in the deep twilight.

"Run," she says, but has no breath to explain why.

The person runs with her and in the parking lot she lunges for the lone car, scrambles to open the nearest door and throws herself inside. The person stumbles in behind her, trying to catch his or her breath.

"Shut the door," she orders, and the person obeys.

"What happened? Are you all right?" It's Elliot's voice. A voice so concerned, so genuinely worried for her that all the defences Kennedy had built up over the course of tonight come crashing down.

"A ... a ... cougar," she says and breaks into loud, uncontrollable crying. Her hands claw the air for something to hold and he's there, letting her pound his back with closed fists and wail into his shoulder.

He doesn't speak, just holds her gently but firmly, and she knows she's finally safe.

20

Kennedy doesn't know how long she's cried for, but knows the swells of emotion could only have subsided in their own time. Somehow she doesn't worry what Elliot might think. As her crying begins to taper off and her stomach finally stops lurching, she falls away from him and against her seat. She is suddenly completely and utterly exhausted and just wants to go home.

"Let me take you home," says Elliot, as if reading her thoughts.

Kennedy nods, wiping at her tear-stained face.

They drive in silence. Only as they pull into the driveway does Kennedy become curious enough to ask the question, "What were you doing in the park?"

"I came to check on you and Sarina at the beach. Sarina said you'd stormed off. She'd tried to call you at home but no one answered. She asked if I'd check the other end of the park."

"But how did you know we were there?" She doesn't recall having mentioned the beach fire to him.

"I have a confession to make. I happen to know how to

listen in on MSN conversations, which I only did," he holds up an apologetic hand, "because I was worried about that Zak guy tracking you. It's also why I went to Video Stop that night."

Another liar, thinks Kennedy, but one with good intentions. "Zak Smith turned out to be my brother Liam's practical joke." She shakes her head. "It's been one insane night." She suddenly wonders what other conversations Elliot may have listened in on. She hopes she hasn't said anything mean about him to Sarina.

"Sarina said you stormed off because of Colin," he says in a quieter voice.

"Colin," she snorts. "Why didn't you tell me what a jerk he is?"

"I thought it was self-evident." He smiles. Kennedy laughs weakly and starts to open the car door.

"Let me help you," says Elliot, getting out his side and hurrying around the car.

"Thanks, Elliot."

The house is dark, not even the front porch light is on. "I wonder if anybody's home?" Kennedy unlocks the door and calls into the dark, "Anybody here?" No answer. Kennedy looks to Elliot. She's too freaked out to be alone right now.

"Would you like to come to my house for a while, until someone's home?" he says. "You probably shouldn't be alone."

"Yeah, I would," she says.

She climbs in the car and he reclines the seat for her. "I'll get you a blanket." He opens the trunk and returns with a blanket, which he tucks in around her, making her feel safe all over again.

"You rest," he says. "It's not far. I'll leave a note on your door with my number, so your parents can call when they get in."

As they step through Elliot's door, his house is filled with the same spicy smells she'd noticed in his car.

Over the sound of television, a woman's voice starts calling out to them in a language Kennedy doesn't understand. Her tone is insistent and bossy, yet has a lilting musicality to it.

"Yes, Grandma, it's me and a friend."

"Kaun saheli hei?" she demands.

Kennedy is led into a small, clean living room, where Elliot's grandmother sits beside a now muted television. She is dressed head to toe in a sari of pink gauzy material. The old woman bats at Elliot's leg, hitting him square on the knee, then stares at Kennedy with eyes the smoky colour of rain clouds. "Kurhi da naan ki hei?"

"This is Kennedy, Grandma. Kennedy, this is my grandmother, Naira."

"Nice to meet you," says Kennedy.

"Ken-ne-dy," she says, drawing out the syllables. "Lumbi?"

"Yes, she's tall for a girl, Grandma. Kennedy, are you hungry?" asks Elliot. "There's hot food."

"Spicy," says the old woman in English. "Lahu lai changa."

Kennedy looks at Elliot and he translates for her. "Naira says Indian food is good for the blood."

"Sounds good, I'm starving," says Kennedy as her stomach rumbles at the smells coming from the kitchen.

"Nice hair," says a woman from the kitchen doorway.

My hair must be wild-looking, thinks Kennedy, smoothing it down.

The woman in the doorway is dressed in black pants and mustard-coloured tunic. Her shiny black hair hangs in a long braid down her back. The measured grace of her movements reminds Kennedy of the first time she met Elliot.

"This is my mother, Emme," says Elliot.

"Hello," says Kennedy. The woman has Elliot's amber-coloured eyes.

Remembering her crying jag, Kennedy wonders if her own eyes are all red and puffy.

"May I use the washroom?" she asks.

"Sure," says Elliot. "I'll show you where it is."

She follows him through the kitchen, thinking he suddenly looks so boyish. And not at all snobbish or full of himself. In the bathroom, she washes her face and wets down her frizz. Looking in the mirror, she doesn't quite recognize herself. Not that she looks different really, it's more that she's seeing herself differently. As if her eyes have been replaced with a fresh pair.

Elliot is sitting at the kitchen table with his mother and Naira's TV is playing in the living room. The food, whatever it is, smells delicious. Kennedy's stomach growls again. She didn't eat any dinner, and what time is it now? She spies a clock over the fridge and is shocked when she sees it's almost ten. Mom's got to be home soon, she thinks, considering it's Tory's bedtime. Probably went out for ice cream or something.

The phone rings and Naira calls out, "Phone." Emme answers, then hands it to Kennedy. "You can talk in private on the porch," she says, gesturing to the door. Kennedy slips outside.

"Hello?"

"Kennedy?"

"Dad! What are you doing home?"

"I," he hesitates, "was a little worried about you, is all, and cancelled my last couple of meetings."

"Worried?"

He changes the subject. "Are you all right? Sarina's left all sorts of messages on the phone, and who's Elliot?"

"I'm fine now. But if you can believe it, I ran into a cougar walking home." Kennedy hears his breath catch in his throat. "I'll tell you all about it when I see you."

"Are you hurt?"

"No, just got scared half to death."

"And where are you?"

"Elliot's. Remember, he's the one who drove Tory and me to the clinic and then to the hospital."

"Oh, yeah. Mom said he seemed like a nice young man."

"He is."

"Shall I come and get you?"

"Yeah. Hold on and I'll find out the address." She asks Elliot for his address and then tells Dad to give her twenty minutes.

"Fine. That'll give me time to clean house a little. It looks as if we've had a minor earthquake."

Mom didn't have time to clean, thinks Kennedy, smiling.

"Kennedy, sweetheart, I love you."

"I love you too, Dad."

"Please sit and I'll give you some food," says Emme when Kennedy's off the phone. Emme has the same calm manner as her son, and Kennedy feels herself relaxing.

She sits in front of a steaming plate of rice, lentils and mushy vegetables that smells like sweet earth. Emme stands behind Elliot and begins to touch his hair, lovingly, as if it's a sacred object. The way he sits, unmoving, Kennedy can tell it's a common occurrence.

"Such beautiful hair you have," Emme says, eyeing Kennedy.

"My mother's a hairdresser," explains Elliot, shaking her hands away from him as if suddenly embarrassed. "She loves hair."

"Pagrhi pawni chahidi," calls the grandmother from the living room. "Hah!"

"Naira has the ears of a bat," says Elliot.

"Ears like dog, not bat," Naira corrects in English.

"Naira is still mad at me for taking off the turban," says Elliot. "She understands English, by the way, just refuses to speak it. So we won't forget our Punjabi."

"How did you meet Kennedy, Elliot?" asks his mom.

"Colin Bernard. He and his mom are staying at Kennedy's."

"Oh, yes."

"Colin, bad boy," calls Naira. "Mara sapp."

"Naira called Colin a mean snake," says Elliot, and Kennedy can't help laughing, a loud boisterous laugh. There's something about Elliot that makes her unselfconscious. He's not judgmental, that's what it is. He's honest and discerning, but not judgmental. She can't think of why she thought him so critical before.

The food feels like health itself and Kennedy eats every last unnameable vegetable despite the fact that she usually hates vegetables unless they're raw and accompanied by a bowl of dip. But then a lot of things have changed today. So why not her taste in food?

She tells them about the cougar, about yelling at it, then singing at it. Their eyes are wide with awe.

"Lucky girl," calls Naira.

"I heard you singing," says Elliot, looking shy suddenly. "You have a fantastic voice, Kennedy."

"Well, the cougar sure didn't like it."

They all laugh, Naira cackling in the other room.

When her dad's car pulls into the drive, Elliot walks her to the door.

"Thanks again, Elliot. For everything," she said.

"No problem." He fidgets with the collar of his shirt. "You still up for going to the opera?" he adds quickly, glancing down at the floor.

"Definitely," she says, and means it. He smiles his great smile.

They say goodnight simultaneously and laugh at themselves. Elliot remains in the doorway, watching her go.

On the drive home, Kennedy tells Dad about the cougar.

"I'll never say you can't take care of yourself," he says when she's finished. "And you know, I think maybe we should listen to Aunt Cathy and cough up the money for a good singing teacher."

"When I get a job, I can help pay for the lessons."

Kennedy walks into the rec room and Colin's there, watching TV on the couch. She has to wonder what happened down at the beach for him to be home this early.

"Hey," he says, cocky as ever, as if he'd done nothing wrong.

"What are you doing here?" Kennedy stops and turns to fix her eyes on his.

"I missed you down at the beach." He pats the couch beside him and Kennedy can't help but snicker.

"You know, Colin, you'll be a lot happier when you start being honest with yourself," she says and he looks at her, dumb, his mouth open. She continues into her room, locking the door behind her with an overt click. She falls onto her bed, her warm inviting bed, and starts kicking off her pants. She's too tired to put on pyjamas and will sleep in her shirt. She's also too tired to read, but as she is drifting off she recalls *Pride and Prejudice*'s great ending. Mr. Bingley tells Elizabeth's sister Jane that he's never stopped loving her and asks for her hand in marriage. And then Mr. Darcy comes to Elizabeth's house and nervously pops the question. By now, Kennedy knows his renewed proposal by heart: *"You are too generous to trifle with me. If your feelings are still what they were last April, tell me so at once. My affections and wishes are unchanged, but one word from you will silence me on this subject for ever."*

"My feelings are quite the opposite," Kennedy says aloud, smiling as sleep overtakes her.

That night, for the first time in years, Kennedy flies in her dreams. She soars high over the forest behind her house, up one side of the mountain and down the other, the warm air rushing past her face, draping her arms and torso like angel hair. Along the beach she can see a fire, bright on the darkened sand, people's pale bodies swimming in the shallows, their voices too distant to pick out their words. Then she notices something else, farther from shore, and has to fly lower to see what she thinks is a seal. But no, it's a cougar, her cougar, paddling its muscled forelegs in the water and huffing noisily through its nose. Its gold eyes reflect on the water like double moons, lighting the way as it pushes onward, seeking out another, friendlier shore.

Acknowledgements

I'd like to thank my children for letting me quote them, Jane Austen for her timeless stories, my husband, Bill Gaston, for his editorial insights, and my insightful and supportive writing group, the LFC. Many thanks to the incisive editing of Elizabeth McLean and to all the staff at Raincoast who are, quite simply, a joy to work with. I'd also like to extend thanks to Emma Baines for her patient help with translating lines into Punjabi. The excerpts from *Pride and Prejudice* are from the Oxford University Press edition (Oxford: Oxford University Press, 1980).

About the Author

Dede Crane lives in Victoria with her husband Bill, their three teenage children, one eight-year-old, two wild cats and a very tame dog. She has published numerous short stories in literary magazines, has been shortlisted for the CBC Literary Award, and is the author of the acclaimed novel *Sympathy*. This is her first work for teens.

By printing The **25 Pains** of **Kennedy Baines** on paper made from 100% post-consumer recycled fibre rather than virgin tree fibre, Raincoast Books has made the following ecological savings:

- 38 trees
- 3, 588 kilograms of greenhouse gases (equivalent to driving an average North American car for eight months)
- 30 million BTUs (equivalent to the power consumption of a North American home for over four months)
- 21, 986 litres of water (equivalent to nearly one Olympic sized pool)
- 1, 343 kilograms of solid waste (equivalent to a little less than one garbage truck load)

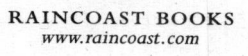

RAINCOAST BOOKS
www.raincoast.com

ANCIENT FOREST
FRIENDLY